The
BATTLE
of the
BLIGHTY
BLING

Ruth Quayle

Illustrated by
Eric Heyman

ANDERSEN PRESS

First published in 2018 by
Andersen Press Limited
20 Vauxhall Bridge Road
London SW1V 2SA
www.andersenpress.co.uk

2 4 6 8 10 9 7 5 3 1

British Library Cataloguing in Publication Data available.

ISBN 978 1 78344 692 6

Printed and bound in Great Britain by
Clays Limited, Bungay, Suffolk, NR35 1ED

To my parents,

Prue and John Quayle – top skippers

CHAPTER
1

My name is Victoria Parrot McScurvy.

Last year my mum and dad sank our pirate ship and lost (nearly) all our treasure.

We used to be the most famous pirates in England. Now we live in a caravan on the south coast, and have a small leaky rowing boat.

Dad says we're the laughing stock of the high seas. Mum says at least we don't get seasick.

My little (I'd say very little) brother is called Bert Parrot McScurvy and our teeny sister is called Maud Parrot McScurvy.

As you can see we all have the same middle name. This is because my parents are lacking in the imagination department. Dad says he likes to keep things simple. Mum says you can't go wrong with a name like Parrot.

Most people just call me Vic.

Bert is extremely small for a pirate. He says he is only one inch smaller than me. That is small. And anyway, he's fibbing.

But he's not as small as Maud. She is tiny.

She's the cutest toddler in the world. Everyone says so. They say 'Butter wouldn't melt' and 'Look at those eyes' and 'What a cutie'.

Bert says he 'j'adores' Maud, and he hugs her too tightly. He thinks this makes her laugh but she's not laughing, it's just that her face is all squished.

Maud likes me better than Bert. Bert doesn't agree. He also thinks he is funny but he's not. So you see, he often gets this kind of thing wrong.

Sisters are much better than brothers.

Maud is so small she sleeps in the sink. In a plastic washing-up bowl that bobs around in the water. She likes to be afloat. We all do.

When we moved here, we got lots of funny looks and whispery comments from the people who live in the neat houses nearby. Once, Bert pulled down his trousers and showed them his bottom. Now they really hate us.

If we hadn't lost our pirate ship, this wouldn't have mattered. We could have made them walk the plank. Or we could have tied them to the mast and let the seagulls eat them.

Losing a ship is the worst thing that can happen to a pirate. You don't just lose your home; you lose all the stuff that matters a lot.

Bert lost a pet shark called Dave. I lost my award-winning collection of lobster claws. Mum lost her favourite pink bikini. Dad lost his marbles.

But Maud was the one who minded the most. Maud lost her nuggy.

Nuggy was Maud's favourite blanket. For five months after our ship went down the only words Maud spoke were 'Want nuggy. Want nuggy'.

Mum and Dad explained to Maud that nuggy was inside our old ship and we couldn't get it back. They stole lots of new nuggies for Maud but she never forgot the real one. Maud is very determined.

We used to sail the oceans. Now we have to wear shoes and do homework. Dad says it's a tragedy. Mum says get a grip.

But we can't get a grip because we don't fit in round here. And the reason people round here look and laugh and chatter about us is because we DON'T LOOK NORMAL. Anyone can see that.

4

Let's start with my mum. She's enormous – six foot, three inches – which in case you don't know is massive for a woman. She's also muscly and has tattoos on her arms. And she always wears short-sleeved party dresses to show them off. She laughs most of the time. She even laughs at Bert when he's not being funny.

Dad is much smaller. He's very skinny and he has long hair and one eye and he gets his left and right muddled up. He doesn't laugh much. Mum says he's a crosspatch.

But Mum and Dad aren't in this story. It's about us children – me, Bert and Maud.

Bert is extremely naughty and he shouts a lot. He thinks he's a better pirate than me just because he has a lazy eye and has to wear an eyepatch. But everyone knows that real pirates don't wear eyepatches. Just the ones in picture books. I sometimes hide his eyepatch. He doesn't laugh then.

Maud has big brown eyes and bright blond hair and she smiles at everyone. But don't let that deceive you. One of her teeth is already rotten because she eats so many strawberry sherbets. She crunches through at least a hundred of them a day. She knows a lot of rude words, and not many normal ones.

But yesterday, when Mum and Dad were out at work, unpacking food at our local supermarket (and nicking the gone-off things for our dinner), something really exciting and actually quite piratey happened to us kids. Bert says it definitely wasn't a dream because we have actual real-life bruises so it has to be true.

We weren't quite on our own because Pedro, our very old parrot, was left in charge. Pedro has a nasty temper and a very sharp peck. Mum says you wouldn't mess with Pedro. Anyway, this is what happened. And like lots of things in our caravan, it started with an argument.

CHAPTER

2

I was playing peekaboo with Maud. It's her second-favourite game. Her absolute best is breaking things. Toys and mugs and stuff I make for her. Dad says it's a sign of good swashbuckling blood. Mum says he's not the one who has to clear it up.

I was quite bored but I couldn't stop because Maud kept biting me on the nose if I tried to walk away.

'It's a sign of love,' I said, trying not to wince.

'It's her rotten tooth,' said Bert.

Then Maud, who was bored, said, 'Wanna

play pirates.'

Bert and I looked at each other. We're not allowed to play pirates. Especially when Mum and Dad aren't here.

Nobody is supposed to know we are pirates. If they found out, they'd probably put us in prison and take away our cutlasses and our rowing boat.

They even (*shhhhhhh!*) might find the Blighty Bling.

The Blighty Bling is a jewel – a very famous jewel. It's an enormous red ruby, the shape and size of an eye, surrounded by tiny diamonds and emeralds that are arranged like a skull. It hangs on an old gold chain and when you wear it around your neck, it's like a third eye, helping you spot ships and rocks and wrecks and desert islands and . . . rival pirates.

Well, this is the idea, although it didn't do Dad much good when our ship, *Sixpoint Sally*, sank. But then again, he wasn't wearing it. At least I don't think he was. Mum and Dad are a bit hazy about the details.

I wasn't on board at the time and nor was Bert. We were staying with Granny McScurvy on her houseboat for retired pirates. We go there for a week every year. Maud was with Mum and Dad because Granny McScurvy refuses to look after her. Granny McScurvy says her nappy days are over. She also says Maud is a Tyrant with a capital T.

Mum and Dad love it when Bert and I go to stay with Granny McScurvy. They say it gives them a break but I think this is a fib. After all they still have to look after Maud. I think it's because they like to go to dangerous places without us. Places like Puffin Island.

I've never been to Puffin Island but I know ALL about it. It's surrounded by the Hammerhead Rocks and every pirate knows that it's a dark and dangerous underworld full of secrets and hidden treasure. It's where lots of pirates go to hang out, meet up and just be piratey – pirates like our old arch-enemy Captain Guillemot the Third. This is where *Sixpoint Sally* sank last year, but I don't know what happened because Mum and Dad won't talk about it. Mum gets twitchy when I ask her to tell us. All she'll say is that if she'd known what Dad was up to we never would have lost our ship and we never would have ended up in a leaky caravan. She gives Dad a look when she says this. I'm not sure why.

Mum was wearing the Blighty Bling when she first met Dad on Brighton Pier twelve years ago. At first, he tried to fight her for it, then he got all soppy and fell in love with her. Mum says he was the first man who thought she was prettier than the Blighty Bling. That's why she married him. Dad says he got two jewels for the price of one.

Every year on their wedding anniversary, Mum puts on the Blighty Bling, Dad pretends to fight her for it, and then they drink too much rum and crash out on the floor. I know this isn't the sort of thing *your* mum and dad do, but for us pirates drinking rum is normal behaviour. We like it better than orange squash.

Anyway, the rest of the year the Blighty Bling stays in a safe place in its pink velvet box. Mum says if anyone saw it they'd put it in a museum, and she doesn't want that because it's been in her family for thousands of years, well, hundreds definitely. Her ancestors won it from the Guillemots during the famous Battle of the South Coast in 1823. And now it's our only remaining bit of treasure and every pirate in Europe, and maybe even the world, would love to get their hands on it. Especially Captain Guillemot the Third who thinks it is his property even though everyone else knows it's ours.

So you get the picture. It's important.

Maud looked at me calmly and placed her hands over her ears. She paused for just a few seconds. Then she opened her mouth.

And she started to . . . SCREAM.

I have to pause here for a bit. Just to blink a few times.

You see, if you've never heard Maud scream before, you can't possibly imagine how bad it is.

Think of a police siren going on and on and on and on and on and on. Right next to your ear just as you're trying to go to sleep at night.

It's way worse than that.

'You said NO to Maud!' said Bert.

'But we're not allowed to play pirates.'

Bert frowned for quite a long time, and then he grinned.

Maud, who was looking at us both, stopped screaming, toddled over to Bert and gave him a hug.

Bert smirked.

'Want to play pirates, Maud?'

She put her thumb in her mouth and looked at me.

'Yeth pleathe.'

Well, what was I supposed to do? I couldn't let her start screaming again, could I? And I absolutely couldn't let her like Bert more than me.

So I went into the caravan.

Luck was on my side because Pedro (remember, he's the parrot with the bad temper who was meant to be in charge) was asleep. He's getting old and needs more sleep than he used to.

I grabbed the cutlasses from the top of the fridge. And just before I climbed down, I took the Blighty Bling out of its pink velvet box and popped it in my back pocket. I don't know why. Well, actually I do. I wanted to impress Maud. I wanted to make her think I was even better at playing pirates than Bert.

I know we're not supposed to touch it, but the thing about being pirates is that we often do naughty things.

We can't help it.

CHAPTER

3

Bert and Maud think sword fighting is all *whack, whack, whack,* but it isn't. It's a fine art. It's about balance and precision. I know this because my dad told me and he used to be one of the best sword fighters in the pirate world.

He won a gold medal for sword fighting in the 2005 Pirate Games. He is very pleased about this because his old arch-rival Captain Guillemot the Third only got silver.

Mum says Dad may have won a gold medal for sword fighting but he managed to lose an entire ship full of treasure and, if she were him, she wouldn't keep boasting about one teeny-weeny useless medal. She's sort of cross when she says this but then she pats him on the shoulder too, which means she isn't really. They're quite confusing, my mum and dad.

Anyway, try telling Bert and Maud that sword fighting is a fine art.

'I deaded you,' Maud shrieked.

'Take that! And that!' Bert specialises in aiming at the belly, then taking a swipe at the top of your head.

We fought for about twenty-six minutes, until I was quite sore and very sweaty.

Then Bert sat on top of me and started whistling. He's very annoying.

I shouted:

'STOP!'

Bert and Maud moaned, they always do, but this time I managed to distract them by suggesting we raid the fridge. We like fridge raids, especially when Mum and Dad are out.

So we left the cutlasses lying on the grass outside, and went in to eat leftover chocolate mousse and loads of sweets. We always eat a lot of crisps and sweets and chocolate. Mum doesn't mind because we're pirates and we're meant to lose teeth. It's one of the best things about being us, although nobody at our school agrees. It's not great when we have to get our rotten teeth pulled out, but Mum gives us an extra big bag of sweets if we don't scream too much – so it's win-win really.

But I wish we'd taken our sweets outside rather than spending so long eating them on the sofa. Because when we finally went out again our cutlasses were gone.

Bert burped. 'They've been taken,' he said. He's not the brightest.

We searched for them all round the field where we live. It is full of thistles and nettles and two old

19

goats that eat everything except the thistles and nettles. Round the field is a wooden fence. And behind it is a beach.

'Off to sea, my hearties!' Bert shouted, racing ahead. He thinks he's so clever.

I gave Maud a piggyback. She kept strangling me, but I didn't mind too much. I really love my little sister.

Our beach doesn't look at all like those beaches you see on postcards or in magazines.

The sand isn't white and the sea isn't blue. It's covered in grey pebbles and old shells and there are fallen-down beach huts and old cafés

that haven't been open for a long time. And all the way along, like rotting dinosaur bones, are wooden breakwaters covered in seaweed. The sea is dirty-grey and on calm days, when it's flat and oily, you can see rubbish floating like dead seagulls on the surface of the water. Sometimes there really are dead seagulls.

One of our favourite games is spotting the best bit of rubbish. Once I found a dirty nappy. It was floating in the water and it had opened up so you could see all the baby poo, which was bright orange. Maud waved at it until it disappeared. Bert's best thing was an old telly, with a seagull sitting on top.

It's a really good beach.

But today we had only one thing on our mind.

Our cutlasses.

'Look.' Bert pointed.

I looked.

Sitting on one of the breakwaters was a girl and a boy. They were very clean and they were wearing fancy-dress pirate clothes. She had on glasses and he had a stripy knitted hat. Their hair was shiny and they were smirking at us.

In their hands were our cutlasses.

'We're pirates,' said the girl, who had red hair. 'So we need these.'

I burst out laughing. Wearing pirate clothes didn't make them pirates. Real pirates wear ripped jeans and shorts and T-shirts with cool pictures on the front. We wear normal-ish clothes, things like hoodies and flip-flops. Maud wears an old party dress that Dad found in a dustbin.

'We're pirates, aren't we?' the girl continued, elbowing the boy.

He nodded and looked at his feet. Underneath his knitted hat, he had very short hair, so you could see all the bumps and veins on his head.

'I'm Captain Blackbird,' she said grandly. 'This is Swashbuckler Robin. Also, we're not just pirates, we're famous too.'

I cleared my throat.

'Give 'em back, or ELSE.'

'GIVE US BACK OUR CUTLASSES!!!'

'Else what? Will you chase us home, will you tell your mum, will you cry like big dirty babies, will you . . .?' She paused to think.

'We'll fight you,' Bert shouted, running at her.

I ran to join him. 'We're the REAL pirates!' I bellowed.

We had to get those cutlasses back. They'd belonged to my great-great-great-great-great-great grandfather, Captain McScurvy the First. They'd been passed down through our family for two hundred years. They'd survived some of the worst battles in pirate history.

But, most important of all, they were the only weapons Mum and Dad had left.

'You're not pirates. You're just lazy layabouts with holes in your shoes and rotten teeth, that's what our mum says you are,' said the girl, who was very pale.

I tripped her up.

Maud clapped. 'Fight, fight!' she said happily.

'Give them *back*,' I said again. 'Those are real pirate cutlasses and no one ever steals a pirate's cutlass. Not even your oldest arch-enemy. If you were real pirates you'd know that.'

It was true. Pirates may be bloodthirsty and greedy and very often quite bad, but there are certain rules that even the most evil swashbucklers stick to.

The girl and boy looked at each other and put our cutlasses behind their backs.

'What's so piratey about you lot?' she said suspiciously. 'All you've got is rusty old cutlasses and one dirty eyepatch between you.'

'Well, at least we're not wearing dressing-up clothes and knitted hats.'

'I'll have you know,' said the girl, 'that Swashbuckler Robin knitted that hat himself. He is a brilliant knitter; he won the county knitting contest.'

'Knitting is for grannies, not for pirates,' said Bert. 'Anyway, we've got a boat.' He pointed to our leaky rowing boat.

The girl burst out laughing.

'If that's a pirate ship, I'm your aunt Gladys.'

'We don't have an aunt Gladys!' Bert shouted.

'I think that's the point,' I told him.

'Huh?'

I told Bert to put a sock in it. Which is pirate for shut up.

'Prove to us that you're real pirates,' the girl said calmly. 'And I'll give them back. But I need proper, solid proof. Not some leaky old rowing boat.'

I paused. For a long time.

We all knew what would prove once and for all that we were real pirates.

I felt in my back pocket and pulled out the Blighty Bling just to make sure it was still there. I kept my hand

hidden behind my back, but then realised Bert and Maud were standing just behind me.

I put the Blighty Bling in my pocket again and gave them a death stare, trying to warn them not to say anything.

But Maud just grinned at me and said in a loud clear voice, 'Blighty Bling, Blighty Bling. It's so sparkly. It's real treasure . . .' She paused, realised what she'd done, and frowned. 'And it's definitely not in Vic's pocket,' she finished, popping a strawberry sherbet in her mouth.

I glared at Maud. She went purple like a boiled beetroot and started to pull faces. She does this when she wants to change the subject and get out of trouble.

But it was too late. The annoying girl was staring at my back pocket with a nosy look on her face.

Our secret was out.

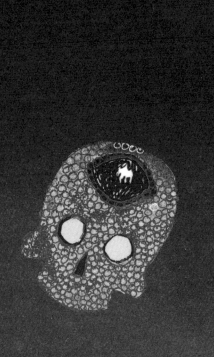

CHAPTER

4

'What is that baby talking about?' asked the girl.

'She's talking rubbish,' I said crossly.

'Show us this Blighty ring thing and you can have your rusty old cutlasses back.'

'Blighty Bling, not Blighty Ring,' Bert interrupted in his most withering voice.

I kicked him.

'Aha,' said the girl. 'So it does exist!'

'S'just a myth,' I tried to tell them, but I am one of those people who goes red when I tell a lie. 'S'just an old pirate legend.'

'You've gone red,' she said laughing. 'You've gone bright red. You're like a tomato.'

I went even redder.

'Just show it to us and we'll give them back.'

We said no once, then we said it again. Then we shouted it a lot more times.

But the girl wouldn't listen. She just kept on and on and on at us until quite a long time had passed and we still didn't have our cutlasses and I was fed up.

I couldn't weaken though, because if there is one rule in our house that even Bert would never break, it is *not talking about the Blighty Bling*.

'You're just pretending,' she said. 'You're not pirates, you've never been pirates, you're just silly scruffy kids with nothing to do but pretend. And you're jealous of our outfits because you could *never* afford ones like this and you can't knit to save your lives. And you're not brave, and you're not tough and I bet you even get seasick and you're the most unpiratey children I've ever met in my life and just wait till our mum tells your mum you've let us play with rusty cutlasses – who will be the big brave pirate kids then?' As she spoke, she looked at me and Bert without blinking.

I tried to laugh but actually I was beginning to feel nervous. What would Mum and Dad say when they got back and discovered we'd lost the cutlasses? And, even worse, when they discovered we'd been telling normal non-pirate children that we were pirates.

But, still, I couldn't have her telling us we WEREN'T real pirates. We do have our pirate pride.

I looked at Bert. He nodded. We were thinking the same thing. We WANTED to show them the Blighty Bling just to shut up this annoying girl with her neat bob and clean fingernails, but we knew deep down that we never could.

I listened to the sea sloshing against the breakwater and a seagull cawing above our heads. I couldn't see a way out.

Then all of a sudden Maud stamped her feet and grinned at everybody.

'I goddit!' she said.

We'd forgotten about Maud.

We'd forgotten that she is only three and, although very cute, is extremely naughty. We'd forgotten that she is so small, she reaches exactly up to the back pocket of my jeans. We'd forgotten that she loves sparkly things.

We'd bloomin' well forgotten to keep an eye on her.

And we hadn't seen her take the Blighty Bling out of my pocket.

She held out her hand and there it was. It gleamed.

For a minute. or so nobody said anything at all. We just stared at it.

It sparkled and shimmered and shone.

'Let me TOUCH IT!' said the girl. 'Come on, bubba. Give it to Arabella.'

(*Arabella!* So that was her real name. YUCK.)

Maud just stuck out her tongue.

'Get it, George!' said Arabella.

The boy twitched. He was pretty big, at least eleven.

But Maud wasn't a pirate baby for nothing. She put the Blighty Bling around her neck and said, 'Farty pants, farty pants!'

'I want that jewel,' Arabella told her brother. 'It will go perfectly in my collection.'

She turned back to us. 'I'm a beachcomber in my spare time. I have an impressive collection of artefacts. One day I might open a museum.'

Bert scowled at her. 'The Blighty Bling will NEVER be in a boring old museum. The Blighty Bling stays in its box in our caravan and that's that.'

Arabella snorted. 'How mean-spirited,' she said, clicking her tongue between her teeth. 'A jewel like this is public property.'

'It's McScurvy property,' I told her. 'So keep your thieving hands off it. We're taking it back to our caravan *right now*. And if I were you, I'd pretend you'd never laid eyes on it. If our mum and dad ever hear you talking about it, they'll feed you to the seagulls.'

Arabella laughed. 'I think they might have more pressing things to worry about first,' she sniggered, pointing towards the sea. 'Their own child for instance!'

I looked in the direction Arabella was pointing and gasped. While we'd been arguing, Maud had toddled off towards our leaky old rowing boat. Now she hopped aboard and picked up the oars.

I shouted:

'Maud!

Come back!'

But Maud just waved. She's a very good rower, especially for a three-year-old. She's a pirate after all. We pirates may not be able to ride bikes or scooters but we learn to row before we can walk. Maud is the best rower in the family. Mum says Maud was born to row.

A moment later, we saw Pedro fly past us, soar towards Maud and land on her shoulder.

Oh great. Pedro could have helped us and ordered Maud to come back, but now he'd flown over to look after Maud. He always favours the littlest person.

Bert and I had to move fast.

There were lots of other boats on the beach, and because we are REAL pirates we chose the best-looking one and pinched it. Well, *borrowed*. Sort of.

We found a coil of rope in one of the lockers on board. It was all we had.

Maud was now a long way out ahead of us. And she seemed to know exactly where she was going.

That was probably because she had the Blighty Bling. And remember what I said about the Blighty Bling? It's like the best map you've ever had; it leads you exactly where you want to go – the quickest route. But where *did* she want to go?

'I've got good news and bad news,' Bert said, looking up at the sky and squinting through his patch-free eye.

I ignored him.

'The good news,' he continued, 'is that this is a

sailing boat. So we can put up a sail and go faster.'

This WAS good news.

'But the bad news is –' he let out a big sigh – 'that's one heck of a storm brewing out there.'

I looked over to where he was pointing.

The sky was turning black and purple. The clouds were racing towards each other and crashing like dodgem cars. It was a massive storm and it was coming towards us fast.

CHAPTER
5

'I have a way with boats,' Bert said breezily. Bert always thinks he has a way with things. He's usually wrong.

'Then why do you keep pulling the sail in when it needs unfurling.'

'You're extracting me,' he said.

'You mean *distracting*.'

'I mean stop being bossy and let me get on with it.'

I let him get on with it.

'Heave ho!' he said finally.

We were under way. But we'd spent so long fumbling that Maud was the size of a seagull in the distance. And she was still rowing as if she knew exactly where she was going. Which was more than I could say about *us*.

'Maud, we're on our way!'

'Don't worry, Maud!'

But the wind picked up our words and threw them back at us.

And, to tell you the absolute honest truth, which I have to confess I don't always do, it didn't look at all as though Maud *needed* our help.

She looked fine. She looked what Mum and Dad would call 'cut-throat'.

The sea was getting pretty rough. It was mostly white from all the spray, and some of the waves looked bigger than our caravan.

If anyone ever tells you that pirates don't get seasick, they're wrong. Real pirates *do* get seasick. And some of them get very VERY sick.

'Blalglghghghghghghgghghghghgh!'

I put my head over the side.

I puked my guts up. Nearly.

Bert looked at me. 'That's the grossest thing I've—' But he couldn't finish what he was saying because soon he was being just as sick as me.

'Urrrrrrrhghghghghghurrrrrrrrrrr!'

It slowed us down a bit because we had to keep leaning overboard to be sick, which meant Maud got further away from us, and we had to work even harder to catch up.

Maud didn't seem to be seasick. She was crunching strawberry sherbets. I could tell because she was leaving a trail of pale pink wrappers behind her.

Pirates have always been litterbugs. It's in our blood.

The black clouds were right above us now. It started to rain and the air changed. It was cold and damp. Far too cold for us in our thin T-shirts. It reminded me of when I was a smaller pirate and we got lost at sea for three weeks and we only had two tins of baked beans and five smelly crabs to eat, and we couldn't see land for days, and Captain Guillemot the Third was after us (because remember what I said about him always trying to steal the Blighty Bling), and we got very cold and

very wet and, well,
I don't mind
admitting,
really quite
scared.

'I don't
believe it,'
Bert suddenly
said, now
pointing.

Behind us, quite a long way back, but getting closer all the time, was a fast motor boat. Sitting behind the wheel, wearing smart bright-orange life jackets and sensible safety harnesses, were Arabella and George. And they were STILL holding our cutlasses.

'We need that boat,' said Bert.

'We need our cutlasses,' I reminded him.

So we turned our boat around, and headed back towards them.

Anyone could see, that from a real pirate's point of view, things were not exactly hearty.

CHAPTER
6

'Ahoy there!' said Arabella, who was taking her 'pretending to be a pirate' game a bit too far.

George, the boy, didn't say anything. His job in life just seemed to be to look pale and big. Arabella did all the talking.

'Need a bit of help, you two?'

George slowed down the engine.

'Where did you steal that boat from?' asked Bert.

'It's our father's pride and joy,' said Arabella. 'And we didn't steal it, we borrowed it. So there.'

'Give us a tow, go on,' I said. 'Our little sister's out

47

there and there's a storm coming.'

'Oooh,' said Arabella in a pretend baby voice. 'Do you brave, strong, savage REAL pirates need help from your old pals George and Arabella?'

'You're not our pals,' growled Bert.

I elbowed him in the tummy.

'Give us a tow!' I said again.

Arabella paused. Our boat swayed over on to its side. The waves sloshed over the bow.

'Only if you say please and ask nicely, like well-behaved children,' she said with a sickly smile.

I cleared my throat and said in a sort of grunt, 'Plse.'

It was the best I could come up with. I'm a pirate. I don't know HOW to be polite.

'Couldn't hear her, could you, George?'

George just stared at us. Arabella cranked up the engine and they began to move away from us. Our boat started to wobble.

'PLEASE!' I shouted.

'I think you can do even better than that,' said Arabella.

'Pretty PLEASE with a huge dollop of candy floss on top,' said Bert, who looked a bit pale.

'Strawberry ice cream,' said George, speaking for the first time.

'George likes ice cream.'

'But it's just an expression, we don't really have any,' Bert said crossly.

'JUST SAY IT,' she hissed.

Our boat swayed.

We both shouted together.

'PRETTY PLEASE WITH A HUGE DOLLOP

OF STRAWBERRY ICE CREAM ON TOP!'

Arabella grinned. 'Welcome aboard, my hearties,' she said. 'And hold on to your hats.'

We weren't even wearing hats. But we climbed aboard, shaking a little, while Arabella tied our boat to hers. Then she got out a toy telescope and turned up the engine to its highest setting.

'All right, shipmates, let's go and find that Blighty Bling,' she said, laughing away. I must admit that as pirates go, she was doing a pretty good job of pretending to be one.

The storm had reached us by now. None of us could speak because the wind just picked up our words and smashed them into the rolling sea. The waves were so large that the boat made a horrible banging sound every time it crashed into one. It felt as though it might smash to pieces. And it was cold too, cold and wet and quite scary.

We raced through the water so fast that it wasn't long before we saw Maud again. Head bobbing, Pedro on her shoulder, big smile on her face.

But far behind her in the distance was something Maud couldn't see.

The moment I caught sight of it, I felt sick. But not in a seasick kind of way.

Up until now things had looked quite bad. But now things looked really, really dangerous. Because sailing behind Maud was a huge black pirate ship. It had a square sail and a tall mast. On top of the mast was a flag and a bird's skull.

Every real pirate knew who that ship belonged to.

And every McScurvy, including me, Bert and Maud, feared it more than anything in the world.

The ship was called *The Raven* and it belonged to Captain Guillemot the Third, Mum and Dad's OLDEST ARCHEST enemy.

We hadn't seen him for a long time. And we hadn't missed him.

He was the last person we wanted to see on a stormy day, far out at sea, without our parents.

Captain Guillemot is known as the scourge of the seas. Some people call him the Hipster Ripster because he loves fashion almost as much as he loves fighting. But don't get distracted by his appearance.

Mum says Captain Guillemot is your basic nightmare. Not JUST because he's big and strong and good at fighting, but because he has something that no other pirate has.

GOLD TEETH. A full set of gold teeth.

You may think you know everything there is to know about gold. But you probably just know that it's valuable and rare and that it shimmers like nobody's business. What you don't know is that gold is also very strong. And this is exactly what makes Captain Guillemot's teeth so dangerous. Believe me when I tell you that when Captain Guillemot chooses to bite somebody, it's not pretty.

My uncle Ray once lost three fingers to Captain Guillemot, just for calling him Fishface.

Captain Guillemot does not like being called names. He doesn't like being laughed at. But it's hard not to laugh at him because he is such poser.

The problem is, if he catches you so much as smirking he'll bite a chunk out of you in next to no time. Dad says he's killed more people than we've had cold dinners – and that's A LOT.

'Now we're really in trouble,' I said.

'What a beautiful boat,' said Arabella.

'Er, helloooo,' Bert said witheringly.

'What a simply exquisite piece of craftsmanship. Utterly fascinating,' she continued. 'It's an old square-rigger. I've studied them at school. What a treat to see one in full sail. What. A. Stunner.'

'A stunner, a stunner!' said Bert, hopping up and down like a frog with ants in his pants. 'I'll stun you! Do you realise who that is behind the ship's wheel? It's only Captain Guillemot the Third, the most fearsome and bloodthirsty pirate of the seven seas. Do you have the teeniest idea what he'll do when he gets wind of the fact that Maud's got the Blighty Bling? DO YOU HAVE A CLUE WHAT IT ACTUALLY MEANS TO BE A REAL PIRATE?!'

'OH, do calm down, little boy,' said Arabella.

Bert turned pink.

'Little?' he gasped. 'I'm only an inch smaller than Vic, and she's two years older. Anyway, my mum says good stuff comes in little packages.'

'Of course she does,' said Arabella in an infuriating, soothing voice. 'But not as good as the stuff in big packages. Look at George.'

Bert stared at George, (who certainly was big for eleven and did look like he was a goody-goody), then he waited till Arabella had turned away, and pulled his most gruesome face at her, tongue out, fingers in his eyes, teeth like a rabbit. George noticed but didn't say anything.

I thought that was quite good of George.

'Do you two want to rescue your sister and this bling thing or not?' called out Arabella over the wind. 'Or do I have to do everything?'

She was right.

I picked up our coil of rope and George turned up the engine.

But we were out of luck.

CHAPTER

7

The problem was, Maud didn't want to be rescued.

When we caught up with her, she just laughed at us and said, 'Go away, poo poo bums.'

If she'd been alone we'd have been fine, we could have picked her up and sailed her home as quick as possible, but she had Pedro with her. And the thing about Pedro is that it's impossible to get near something that he decides to protect.

In this case, I didn't know whether he was more interested in protecting Maud or the Blighty Bling. But either way, it was impossible.

Every time I tried to grab Maud, Pedro flapped his wings at me, squawked loudly and pecked me with his sharp beak.

Then he said, in his nasty parroty voice, 'Go away, poo poo bums. Go away, poo poo bums.' Because, like any parrot, he tends to repeat things. And he likes rude things best of all, which isn't surprising really, he's lived with us lot since he was just a parrot chick.

'Nuggy,' smiled Maud happily, not seeming to notice the storm raging around her small leaky boat. 'Nuggy, nuggy, nuggy.'

I swallowed.

Of course. That's where Maud was heading.

Remember what I said about Maud losing her nuggy when our ship sank last year? And remember that I said Maud refused to give up on nuggy. Well, now I knew why she'd taken the Blighty Bling and headed out to sea. Maud was on a mission to find her long-lost nuggy. And she was going to use the Blighty Bling to show her the way.

This wasn't good.

'She's not going to come back until she's found her nuggy.'

'Her what?' said Arabella.

'Her special blanket,' snapped Bert. 'She can't live without it.'

'Are you telling me,' said Arabella, 'that a three-year-old would take your Blinky ring thing, and come all the way out here in a storm to find a grotty old blanket?'

'S'not grotty, s'lovely!' shouted Maud.

'You've forgotten she's a pirate baby,' I said.

'And she's even naughtier than me,' Bert said proudly.

Arabella looked impressed.

'I'm starting to think you lot might be a lot more piratey than you look,' she said.

'We ARE,' I told her. 'And that huge ship over there, the one you are so impressed with, that belongs to our old arch-enemy Captain Guillemot the Third and if we're not careful he will capture us all and chew us into tiny pieces with his gold teeth. I mean it.'

'Right,' said Arabella, thinking hard. 'So we're going to need a plan then.'

'I want my mum,' said a voice. It was George. He still looked big, but now he was even paler than before and he looked pretty scared.

'It's all right, George,' said Arabella. 'We're cleverer than pirates. We've got a private tutor, remember? We just need to have a good long think about how to outwit that big baddie over there.'

'There's no time for a long think,' Bert spluttered. 'Pirates don't sit around and think and do sums and write poetry. They fight. And that's what we've got to do – fight.'

60

'Oh, honestly,' said Arabella, 'your methods are so outdated. What's the point of fighting if the thing you're fighting for has done a runner right in front of your eyes?'

Bert stopped.

I looked up.

Sure enough, while we'd been bickering, Maud had dipped her oars back into the water and was, once again, a speck in the distance and heading off towards an island on the horizon. Without us.

And changing course and closing in on her fast was Captain Guillemot, his fearsome pirate crew and his enormous black ship, *The Raven*. He was looking at Maud through a telescope. His gold teeth glittered like treasure. Captain Guillemot was smiling. He had obviously spotted the Blighty Bling.

'Switch on the engine, George!' Arabella and I ordered at exactly the same time.

And we raced through the waves towards Maud.

CHAPTER

8

By the time we caught up with Maud again, the storm had started to blow itself out. The wind became less strong, the waves got smaller, Bert and I stopped shivering in our thin T-shirts – and we could speak in normal voices again. Even Maud seemed calmer. She stopped rowing and looked quite pleased to see us. She waved an oar. ''Ello Vic, 'ello Bert. Can I have a biscuit?'

So that's why she was so pleased to see us. All that rowing had made her hungry.

'Maud!' shouted Bert. 'Look behind you!'

Maud had been concentrating so much on rowing, she hadn't seen *The Raven* approaching. She hadn't seen Captain Guillemot.

Captain Guillemot was now only about fifty metres from Maud's boat and he was getting closer all the time. He stood at the front of his boat and pushed out his chest.

He had greasy black hair which he wore in a bun on the top of his head and a blackish beard on his face. Around his forehead was a red bandana, embroidered with a tiny black skull and crossbones. His jeans were turned up at the ankle. He wore a stripy T-shirt with the word 'DUDE' written across his chest, and he had a very smart black leather waistcoat. On his arm he had a tattoo of himself and a large red heart.

He was the trendiest pirate on the planet.

He was also massive.

'Yup,' said Bert. 'That's the Hipster Ripster all right.'

'Golly gosh,' interrupted Arabella. 'I've never seen a pirate before.'

Bert jumped up and down.

64

'You've seen *us*,' he spluttered.

Arabella giggled. 'Yes, but I mean *real* pirates. Real proper ones. Ones with a ship and beards and bandanas and . . . evil eyes.'

Behind Guillemot stood three other pirates who were even bigger than him. There were two men and a woman and they each held a cutlass.

Maud frowned.

'Who's that horridish man?' she said. 'Why are his teeth yellow?'

I swallowed. 'Maud,' I said. 'That horridish man is our old arch-enemy Captain Guillemot and his teeth aren't yellow, they're gold.'

Maud narrowed her eyes and looked at Captain Guillemot more closely.

'He's not very lovely,' she announced. 'I don't like him.'

Captain Guillemot was now so close to us he heard what Maud said.

'I AM lovely,' he said. 'I'm gorgeous. Look at my hairy chest, look at my suntan, look at my muscles. Look,' he continued proudly with a nasty grin, 'at my gold teeth.'

'Gold teeth are yucky,' said Maud. 'I only like black teeth.' She paused thoughtfully. 'You're very old. Are you going to die soon?'

Captain Guillemot nearly fell off his ship.

'I'm not OLD!' he roared. 'Everyone says I look young for my age. Don't they, Beefster? Don't they,

Cath? Don't they, Bones?'

He elbowed his crew members.

All three of them nodded so much they looked like the Punch and Judy puppets we saw on the beach last summer. Except they weren't funny. They were scary.

Beefster was as fat as a sumo wrestler. He had a shaved head and he wore yellow swimming trunks that were about ten sizes too small. Cath had blond hair in plaits, bright red lipstick, ripped denim shorts and a red vest. Around her neck she wore a collection of teeth on a gold chain. Bones was thin and ratty-looking with long greasy blond hair, a filthy waistcoat and a sharp, pointy nose.

Captain Guillemot showed us his biceps. 'Look at me!' he said. 'I mean LOOK. AT. ME.'

Maud put her head to one side and looked at Captain Guillemot.

'You're a silly billy.' She giggled.

Bert and I gasped. What was Maud DOING? She was crazy. We knew what Captain Guillemot was capable of. I kept thinking of all the people he had made walk the plank. I kept thinking of the torture chamber he kept below deck. I kept thinking of Uncle Ray's three missing fingers.

Captain Guillemot did not like being called a silly billy.

'Right, you little rascals! I've had enough of you. I've been sailing all night and I need my beauty sleep . . .'

Bert and I sniggered. Captain Guillemot glared at us.

Then he turned back to Maud. 'First of all,' he said nastily, 'you're going to hand over that pretty little jewel because I want it and I need it and it belonged to MY family first – and I'm bigger than you. So there.'

Captain Guillemot leaned towards Maud's rowing boat and held out his hand. 'Come on, you little ankle-biter, hand over the Blighty Bling and I'll let you go back to your brother and sister. But you've got to do it right now or I WILL GET CROSS. And believe me, you do not want me to get cross!'

Come on, Maud, I prayed, *give him the Blighty*

Bling. It might be a famous jewel and everything and it might have been in our family for hundreds of years but I knew it didn't matter as much as getting our little sister back.

Maud shook her head. Maud laughed. Maud said,

'NO!'

Arabella, George, Bert and I gasped.

'Don't be an idiot, Maud,' hissed Arabella.

'Don't call our sister an idiot,' I said.

'But that man is stark staring mad. He'll eat her for breakfast.'

'I love babies for brekkie,' drawled Captain Guillemot. 'They go EXCEEDINGLY well with pancakes.'

I kicked Arabella and told her to shut up because she wasn't exactly helping, but she didn't notice.

'Gosh,' she whispered. 'A pirate and a cannibal. He really IS a baddie.'

'This isn't some joke,' I hissed. 'This is a life-and-death situation.'

'It's certainly very exciting, isn't it, George?'

George didn't answer. He just stared at Maud with a worried look on his face.

'Hand it over to the big bad pirate, Maudie,' I tried again. 'Then we can all go home for some bubblegum ice cream.'

I tried not to think what Mum and Dad would say when we told them we'd lost the Blighty Bling.

But it was better than going home without Maud. I know Maud is a menace but that's the way we like her.

Maud didn't listen.

'I want my nuggy,' she said.

'I'm going to count to three, you imbecile toddler,' shouted Captain Guillemot, 'and if you don't hand me the Blighty Bling, that's it.'

'One!'

Maud did not move.

'Two!'

Maud pulled a face.

'THREE!'

Maud blew a raspberry.

'**THAT'S IT!**' bellowed Captain Guillemot. 'I warned you!'

Captain Guillemot took a flying leap into Maud's boat. Water sploshed over the side. He grabbed hold of Maud.

'Go away!' she screamed. 'Buzz off, you big bully.'

For a moment it was hard to see what was happening because the boat was rocking so much.

Luckily all the shouting disturbed Pedro.

Pedro flew straight at Captain Guillemot's face. He shouted rude words at the top of his parroty voice. He opened his sharp beak, ready to peck.

But Guillemot simply swiped his cutlass at Pedro. Brightly coloured feathers flew up in the air.

'Get over here,' he shouted to his crew. 'Help me, you idiots! Get the Blighty Bling off the brat.'

Beefster, Bones and Cath jumped aboard. They started to grab at Maud, who was wailing loudly.

She held on tight to the Blighty Bling. The boat rocked dangerously.

Meanwhile Guillemot grabbed Pedro by the legs.

'I HATE birds,' he continued nastily. 'I hate their skinny legs and their nasty splatty poo.'

He handed Pedro to the fat pirate in swimming trunks.

'Give it your best throw, Beefster,' he ordered.

'STOP!' shouted Bert.

I tried to shout too but nothing came out of my mouth.

'That's animal cruelty,' said Arabella. 'I'll report you. You could go to prison for this.'

Beefster just laughed.
He grabbed Pedro's
skinny parrot legs
and swung him
round and round
in the air until he
was just a circle
of blurred
colours.

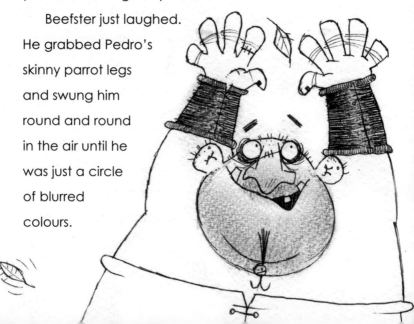

Then he let go and flung poor Pedro far out to sea.

Pedro sailed through the air for a long time.

Then . . . *PLOP!*

He landed in the water with a big splash.

I waited a few seconds, expecting our old parrot to bob up to the surface again, like we do when Mum throws us in the sea for time out. But there was no sign of him.

'Fish food,' said Guillemot, slapping the fat pirate on the back. 'Nice throw, Beefster.'

Maud started to cry.

Bert and I couldn't look at each other.

Losing Pedro was way worse than losing my lobster-claw collection. I know he's a grumpy old boy. I know he never does what he's told. I know he shouts at us and bosses us around. I know he pinches our crisps. But, the thing is, I've known Pedro all my life. Mum said he used to perch on my hammock and watch over me when I was a baby. He used to change my nappy with his beak.

He is a real living thing. He's a crosspatch all right but, the thing is, he is OUR crosspatch.

Or rather he WAS our crosspatch. It was obvious to all of us that Pedro had drowned.

I blinked and felt tears run down my cheeks.

'Vic!' shouted Bert.

I looked up. Captain Guillemot was about to jump back on to his ship and he was holding our sister. Maud bit and scratched and screamed but she was no match for a fully grown pirate like Guillemot.

'Get closer!' I shouted to Arabella.

'I can't,' she said, pulling hard on the ship's wheel. 'The wash from his ship is pushing us out.'

'He's getting away!' shouted Bert. I could tell from his voice that he was nearly in tears.

Captain Guillemot swung Maud over his sweaty shoulder and jumped back on board *The Raven*.

'Give her back!' Bert and I shouted together.

We'd already lost Pedro, we couldn't lose Maud too.

But Captain Guillemot just grinned. His gold teeth flashed.

He squinted at his reflection in the blade of his cutlass and adjusted his carefully arranged bandana.

'The Blighty Bling is back where it belongs,' he said to his crew, who were climbing aboard *The Raven*. 'The McScurvys are finished!'

Guillemot popped Maud up on his shoulders and set off like the clappers.

His roars of laughter were even louder than her screams.

CHAPTER 9

'George!' I shouted. 'Turn on the engine.'

George nodded and pressed some buttons. Our boat jumped into action.

'Good work,' I said, grabbing the ship's wheel.

Arabella peered down her telescope.

'The storm is over,' she said. 'We'll easily catch them. Engines are faster than sails.'

I shook my head. 'Don't you believe it,' I told her. 'A pirate ship in full sail is as fast as any motor boat. Faster, probably. We need to step on it.'

Our engine was so loud, we couldn't hear each

other speak. So for a few minutes we didn't bother trying. We just focused on keeping *The Raven* in our sights. Sometimes we would get close enough to hear pirate laughter. But then Guillemot would roar at his crew to tighten the mainsail and hoist the spinnaker – and *The Raven* would drift further away from us again. Occasionally we spotted a flash of blond hair. It was the only sign we had that Maud was still alive.

Then Arabella called out.

'Look!' she said, pointing into the distance. 'Seagulls. Hundreds and thousands of seagulls!'

I grabbed the telescope. Arabella was right.

Ahead of us was an enormous swarm of birds and they were swooping towards us.

Except I knew at once that they weren't seagulls.

They were puffins.

We all stared at the birds.

'This many puffins,' I said, gritting my teeth and looking back through the telescope, 'can only mean one thing . . .'

Bert leaped to his feet and grabbed the telescope from me.

'Oh no,' he gasped, swallowing like mad and looking crosser than ever. We looked at each other and nodded.

Although we'd never actually been there, we both knew there was only one place in the world that was home to this many puffins . . .

Puffin Island.

And we were heading right towards it.

'What a little oasis!' gasped Arabella.

I saw what she meant. The beaches on Puffin Island were exactly the sort of beaches you see on postcards and in magazines.

White sand, blue lapping water, swaying spiky grass, a gentle trickling stream. And about seventy billion screeching puffins.

'Don't be fooled,' I told her. 'Puffin Island may look pretty but it's just a front. Behind the picture-perfect stuff lies a dark and dangerous underworld, that's what Mum says.'

81

'It's absolutely stunning,' Arabella continued.

Bert wiped his nose on her sleeve.

Then he kicked the side of the boat.

'She'll soon see,' Bert muttered. 'Oasis, my bottom. There's more to this place than sunbathing and surfing.'

Bert doesn't know how to surf. He was only little when Mum and Dad taught me. It was when we were in the Caribbean (we love it there, excellent conditions for sailing and burying treasure). They used to get up before breakfast, borrow some boards from the surf shop, head to the waves, get dunked about a thousand times, laugh like crazy, then give up. Then they fell asleep in the sun and woke up all burnt and blistered. Dad said never again. Mum said don't be a sissy.

Anyway, there's not much chance of surfing these days, not much chance of boating full stop. I suppose this is why Dad doesn't laugh much any more.

Arabella tapped me on the shoulder.

'Stop daydreaming,' she said. 'They're getting

82

away. They're sailing round that corner.'

Arabella was right. While I'd been thinking of the old days, Captain Guillemot had got halfway around the headland.

'We mustn't lose him!' I told the others. 'Turn up the engine.'

We sped so fast over the waves, our boat seemed to crack and shudder. It sounded as if it might break into a thousand tiny pieces.

But we didn't care. We had to catch up with Guillemot. We had to find our sister.

We saw *The Raven* turn and disappear behind some large rocks at the bottom of a steep cliff. I steered our boat through the choppy wake left behind by Guillemot's ship. It was like we were following the larger boat's footprints. I felt sure that if we kept following this trail of foamy sea, we'd eventually catch sight of our sister again. We steered left past the large rocks. The water was choppier here and we held on tight as we rounded the corner. I kept my eyes peeled for Captain Guillemot and began to feel hopeful.

Soon we'd have *The Raven* in our sights again. We'd be able to see where he was taking Maud. But no matter how hard I looked I still couldn't see anything. So I picked up the telescope. And then I had a nasty surprise. Because there in front of us was . . .

. . . absolutely NO PIRATE SHIP.

We all gasped.

The Raven had disappeared.

'She was right in front of us,' said Bert.

He sounded furious, but I know he was more worried than cross. We both were. Once Guillemot had got the Blighty Bling off Maud, he wouldn't need her any more. He'd either chew her into a hundred pieces or take her to his torture chamber or feed her to the sharks. She was only three.

'They *can't* have disappeared,' said Arabella. 'People don't just disappear off the face of the earth – or the sea – not even legendary pirates with spit-spot sailing boats.'

We stood on deck, turning slowly, looking all around us, completely confused. Our boat bumped gently along through the waves. The storm had passed and the day was brightening up. Mum would have said there was just enough blue sky to make a pirate half a pair of knickers. Then she would have said, 'Shame about the other half' and fallen overboard laughing.

But Mum wasn't here.

We looked again. How had we managed to lose him?

I tried to remember things that we'd learned in geography at school but when it comes to tracking down missing pirate ships, school geography isn't much use.

Arabella was right. We were useless pirates. We'd lost our cutlasses to two non-pirate children who had a private tutor. We'd lost our parrot. We'd lost our family's only remaining piece of treasure. Even worse, we'd lost our baby sister.

And we had no idea how to get her back.

I looked at Bert. He looked at me. Sometimes, just sometimes, things are so bad that there doesn't even seem to be any point in fighting your brother.

This was one of those times.

I thought back to the good old days when Bert and I would sit up high in the crow's nest, all sunburnt and happy, looking out for enemy ships and spotting seabirds and dolphins and turtles in the churning sea below. I thought of singing sea shanties under the stars and how we used to tie old bottles to long pieces of string, throw them overboard and pretend we were taking our pets for a walk. And I thought of how easy being a pirate had seemed when Mum and Dad were around deciding what to do.

If only Mum and Dad were here now, I thought, they'd know what to do. Or, rather, they'd pretend to know what to do. Which is kind of as important as actually knowing.

'Righto,' said a loud, booming voice. 'Who's with me?'

For a hopeful minute I thought the voice belonged to Mum.

But it didn't. Of course it didn't. Our mum was stacking shelves at the supermarket, planning what to nick for our dinner. Our mum had no idea we were all the way out at sea and had lost all the things she cared about. Anyway, if she had known she would be shouting a LOT louder than that.

No. The voice belonged to Arabella. And, as usual, she seemed to know exactly what to do. She wasn't even pretending.

Bert and I shrugged. What choice did we have?

'Right,' she said. 'If we stick together, we'll do so much better. Teamwork you see, my hearties.'

I couldn't look at Bert. I knew we'd have to either start giggling, or thump her – and there was no point in doing either of those things. We needed to hear her plan.

Arabella cleared her throat.

'There's no way a square-rigger ship, an entire pirate crew and a loud and naughty three-year-old girl could just disappear,' she said. 'We were only about five minutes behind them. So we just have to sail all the way round the island until we find them. Not very complicated.'

She made it sound so easy.

CHAPTER
10

There are certain things you won't know unless you're a pirate.

Like how to tickle a shark or which bit of a jellyfish is poisonous.

Pirates also know that the sea can lie. I'm not saying it fibs exactly (I'm not that crazy) I'm just saying we know not to trust it. Distances at sea LOOK like they're near but when you actually try to swim or sail to them, you discover they're miles away.

Once, when I was about four, we were out for a sail when Dad saw France on the horizon. He said:

'Let's pop over for lunch. We can try snails.' We all shouted, 'Wee' because that's French for yes. Then we set off across the English Channel. Only trouble was, France was a lot further away than it looked. We didn't get there for lunch. We didn't get there for supper. It took us all day and all night and we got so hungry we had to eat limpets. Mum said they were a bit like snails. I thought they tasted of snot.

Anyway, my point is, it's easy to get timings wrong at sea. Every sailor knows that. Which just proves Arabella isn't really a sailor. She swore it would only take ten minutes to sail the whole way round Puffin Island. I told her it would take at least half an hour. Turns out I was wrong too.

It took us two hours and fifty-three minutes (we timed it on Arabella's water-resistant sports watch).

To begin with it was OK. We had the sun on our faces and the wind in our hair. We were excited to be at sea and hopeful we'd find Maud.

We felt sure she was just around the next headland.

There were seals and puffins and flying fish. The turquoise sea sparkled in the sun. We spotted palm trees and swamps and old ruins. We saw hundreds of sandy beaches.

It felt a bit like the old days.

But being at sea is hard work. For a start there is the steering. Most people think this looks easy. But believe me, it isn't. You know that feeling when you have to run the cross country race at school and your legs actually ache so much they sting? Well, steering a boat for nearly three hours is like this but a hundred times worse. And it's not just your legs that hurt, it's your whole body.

After a few hours, we were in agony. Our eyes were bloodshot from looking into the sun, our arms ached from taking turns holding the wheel, our thighs shook from not being able to sit down and our ears were sore from the constant wind.

On top of all this we were covered in sunburn.

But we knew we couldn't stop because if we did we risked sailing on to some rocks and sinking. We had to concentrate ALL THE TIME.

Even worse than the physical pain was the disappointment of not finding Maud. Each time we came round a fresh headland we felt sure we were going to spot *The Raven* anchored up. Then, when we saw nothing but sea and sand and rocks, our hopes fell as quickly as the weight on one of our crab lines.

Seals and palm trees weren't much good to us when the only thing we wanted to see was a grubby blond three-year-old with a priceless heirloom around her neck.

We sailed the whole way round Puffin Island and we didn't catch one glimpse of Maud.

By the time we got back to where we had started, we were almost too tired to talk. Which was lucky because none of us was actually speaking to each other.

We switched off the engine and bobbed in the water between a pretty beach and the open sea.

92

We were sore and tired. We were fed up. Even worse, we were hungry.

Being hungry may not seem a big deal to you but if you're a pirate you'll understand.

We pirate children are not pleasant at the best of times but when we're hungry we're really bad.

Bert and I hadn't eaten a single thing since our fridge raid that morning. We were ravenous. So we did what we always do when we're hungry. We had a fight.

I blamed Bert for agreeing to play pirates with Maud in the first place. Bert blamed me for taking the Blighty Bling out of its box. I pulled his trousers down, he twisted my nose.

Arabella pulled us apart.

'Stop it!' she said crossly. 'We're trying to find your sister. You can't just give up. What on earth's the matter with you?'

'We're starving,' moaned Bert, clutching his tummy.

Arabella shook her head. 'Exaggerating as usual.' She sighed. 'People who are starving are far

93

too malnourished to moan. You two aren't starving, you're just a bit peckish. But don't worry,' she said, sounding very pleased with herself, 'George and I brought a packed lunch.'

She winked at George. He opened their rucksack and pulled out a Tupperware container.

'Look!' said Arabella. 'Celery, carrot and cucumber, hummus with pitta and an apple for pudding. All our favourite things.'

Bert and I didn't know whether to laugh or cry. We were more starving than we had ever been in our whole lives and the only food available was . . . HEALTHY. We're not supposed to eat healthy food. Mum won't let us. She says you can't trust things that grow in the ground.

We hesitated for about two and a half seconds.

Then we stuffed our faces. Because when you're starving, even healthy food is better than nothing. And, anyway, Mum wasn't there.

I was just crunching my seventeenth carrot stick and thinking it was actually quite tasty when I heard something that made me spit it out and jump to my feet.

'Listen,' I hissed at the others. 'LISTEN!'

All four of us held our breath. Half a minute later, we heard it again, and it was coming from the direction of the beach.

It was the sound of pirates laughing and it made my blood run cold. Because when a pirate laughs you can be sure of one thing – he is doing something VERY bad.

'Did you hear that?'

The others nodded.

'Sailing around the island was a waste of time,' I said. 'They've been here all along. They must have a secret hiding place.'

There was only one thing for it. We had to go ashore.

CHAPTER

11

'Paradise,' said Arabella dreamily when we reached the beach and jumped out on the silky warm sand. 'Utter paradise.'

'It won't feel like paradise when you're being tortured,' I snapped. 'We have to find Guillemot before he finds us. Can anyone hear them?'

But all we could hear was the sound of waves lapping at the shore and a solitary seagull flapping its wings. The laughter had stopped.

'It was definitely coming from this beach,' I said. 'They must be nearby.'

We spread out and searched everywhere – between sand dunes, under boulders, behind trees.

I tried to think of all the things Mum and Dad had told us about Puffin Island. But I realised I didn't know much. That's because they tend to change the subject when we ask about it. They don't like to be reminded of the time *Sixpoint Sally* sank.

The problem was the beach was one long stretch of white sand. There was nowhere to hide a full-size pirate ship.

I wandered down to the sea to join the others. The water in the bay was almost flat calm now. I skimmed a few stones. I didn't have a clue what to do.

'Vic!' shouted Bert. 'Over here.'

Bert, who was up to his knees in water, started jiggling excitedly as if he needed a wee.

I ran over to him. Arabella and George followed.

Bert pointed to a piece of crinkly pale pink plastic that was floating in the sea. Behind it was another, exactly the same. Then another and another. There was a long line of them leading from the beach out into the bay. They went as far as I could see.

Arabella picked one up and held it carefully in her outstretched hands.

'What is it?' she asked.

Bert and I looked at each other. We knew exactly what it was.

'This,' said Bert, looking pleased with himself, 'is very good news.'

He paused for effect, checking he had our full attention.

'This,' he continued, grinning widely, 'is an important clue. And I, Bert Parrot McScurvy, have found it ALL BY MYSELF.'

Bert did a couple of cartwheels. I tripped him up.

'Stop showing off,' I told him, 'and get on with it.'

Bert puffed out his chest. He looked at Arabella and George.

'This,' he said, holding out his palm and showing them the pale pink thing, 'is a sweet wrapper.'

Arabella looked blank. 'So?'

'So,' said Bert, clearing his throat and ignoring her. 'This is not just any sweet wrapper, this is a strawberry sherbet wrapper. And there's only one person on the entire planet who eats this many strawberry sherbets.'

We all started to smile, even George.

'Maud!'

If Maud was dropping sweet wrappers out of Captain Guillemot's ship then surely all we had to do

was follow the trail and we'd find our sister.

We jumped back on board our boat. George switched on the engine.

There was no time to lose.

CHAPTER
12

We followed the strawberry sherbet wrappers slowly at first, then more quickly.

They led us towards a steep cliff that jutted out from the side of the beach.

We listened out for pirate voices.

But instead we heard something you never want to hear at sea, something worse than screaming, worse than a dentist's drill, something worse than a fingernail against a blackboard. Something that sailors are even more scared of than pirates.

It was the sound of our boat scraping against

a rock.

Arabella shrieked. The veins in George's head started to throb. Bert said exactly what I was thinking.

'The Hammerhead Rocks!'

The Hammerhead Rocks are legendary. They surround Puffin Island and thousands of pirate ships have been wrecked on them, including our own ship, *Sixpoint Sally*, we think. The thing about the Hammerhead Rocks is that they are hidden just under the surface of the water so you can't see them. At least, not until it's too late. You need special maps to know where they are. Or you need the Blighty Bling.

We didn't have either.

We reversed our boat and checked for damage. Luckily there was no hole, just minor scrapes, but we couldn't risk going any further. If we sank our boats, we had no way of getting back to the mainland.

So we put down the anchor.

Then we strapped our cutlasses and rope on to our backs and we got ready to swim.

I promise I'm not boasting when I say that Bert and I are Olympic-standard swimmers. We really are.

Cross my timbers. Ask my mum. We're pirates, after all. When we were dribbly little babies, Mum dropped us into the freezing-cold Atlantic Ocean. Then she held up a giant-sized lollipop and said we could have the whole thing for breakfast if we swam back to the boat. It worked. When she did it for Maud, Maud did two miles of butterfly. She was only six months old.

Arabella and George, on the other hand, were doing a lot of splashing but not moving very much because they were still wearing their life jackets.

Arabella puffed. 'I'm in the top class at swim school, I'm just not very used to tides. That's all!'

Well, of course she wasn't used to tides. Normal people only do the normal type of swimming, in swimming pools and leisure centres. They're not used to waves and surf and limpets and seaweed. They're not used to the cold.

Anyway, the thing is, Bert and I had to go back and tow Arabella and George behind us. They were as useless as floating rubber dinghies – and just as heavy.

Luckily the strawberry sherbet wrappers were easy to spot. We followed them into a calm pool, a sort of mini saltwater lake.

We pulled Arabella and George towards us so they could hang on to a rocky ledge. They looked pale.

'I'm really absolutely fine,' Arabella spluttered breathlessly. 'You didn't need to come back for me.'

But she smiled at us anyway.

We all looked up to see if we could make out what was in front of us. This wasn't a hundred per cent easy because it was dark in this pool, despite it being daytime. There was a nasty cold feeling in the air.

It wasn't nice.

'I don't like it here,' shivered Bert. 'It feels all wrong.'

'Hmmm,' said Arabella, who had got her breath back. 'I know what you mean. It does feel wrong, which actually makes me think it's probably right. Pirates don't hide in nice sunny spots, do they? They find the darkest, creepiest of hiding places.'

She put her arm round George. He had gone even paler than usual.

But when our eyes had adjusted to the darkness we found ourselves staring into something REALLY horrible. At the far end of the pool was an enormous, gaping, dark hole.

And everyone knows what a hole in the rock is. You don't need to be a pirate to know about CAVES.

This was the biggest cave I've ever seen. Think of a double-decker bus. No, forget that. Think of three double-decker buses. Now imagine them all piled on top of each other. That's how tall and wide the mouth of this cave was. Three massive London buses wouldn't have even touched the sides of the rock.

But this wasn't one of those caves you can walk in to. No way. You wouldn't be able to. This one had water running straight through it like a river. In other words, a large ship could sail through the mouth of the cave and hide away from the rest of the world.

Arabella let out a deep sigh. 'Well,' she said, 'I didn't know caves could be this huge. And I've never seen one with water running right through it. How very remarkable. How . . .' She paused and looked at us, '. . . how very, very creepy.'

I knew exactly what she meant. The combination of darkness and cold was bad enough, but there was something else that really made us shiver to our bones.

It was the sound of pirates laughing and it was coming from deep inside the cave.

Bert pulled himself up on to the rocky ledge.

'Maud,' he shouted. 'Maud!'

I put my hand over his mouth. 'Be quiet,' I hissed at him. 'If Guillemot finds out we're here, we have zero chance of rescuing Maud. He'll just capture us too.'

Bert wriggled free but he didn't say anything else. He didn't dare.

We all listened hard and heard laughter and singing and shouts spilling out of the cave like an unpleasant smell.

'They're having a party,' I said. 'We have to get Maud out of there before things get out of hand.'

Believe me, pirate parties ALWAYS get out of hand.

'And how are we going to do that exactly?' said Bert. 'Ask very nicely if they'll give her back? I don't think so.'

'Well, what do you suggest then?'

Bert glared at me. He didn't know either.

I didn't say anything for a while. I was too busy thinking.

Then came a new burst of pirate laughter that flew through the cave like canon fire.

It made us all jump.

This was followed by a different sort of sound. It was quieter.

'Did you hear that?' I asked the others.

They shook their heads.

'Listen!' I said. 'There it is again.'

They all looked blank.

'Listen harder,' I told them.

We held our breath.

'I heard it that time,' whispered Arabella. 'But it was just a sigh or something.'

I grinned. 'Exactly,' I said. 'Except I don't think it's a sigh.'

We listened again.

'Is it a moan?' said Arabella.

'Or a burp?' suggested Bert.

George just frowned.

'It's not a sigh or a moan and it's not a burp either,' I told them excitedly. 'It's a yawn.'

I looked at their faces, expecting them to be as thrilled as I was, but they stared at me blankly.

'Don't you get it?' I said. 'A yawn can only mean one thing. They're getting tired. We obviously can't go in there while they're awake but what if we wait till they've gone to sleep?'

Arabella shivered and shook her head.

'Not on your nelly,' she said. 'That means waiting here until they go to bed. Bedtime is hours away. George and I can't possibly wait that long. Our parents will notice if we don't come back for supper. They'll call the police and make a terrible fuss and they'll be sick with worry too. We're just not the sort of children who stay up all night. We have a strict routine.'

Although Arabella's legs and body were under the water, she still managed to look as though she was a school prefect.

I ignored her.

'I didn't say we have to stay out here all night,' I said. 'If you understood the habits of pirates even the teeniest bit you'd know that there is one thing pirates ALWAYS do without fail every afternoon.'

I expected Arabella to have a guess, but for once she didn't seem to have a clue.

Bert did though. A big smile spread across his face.

'Of course!' he said. 'Why didn't I think of that?'

'Because you're lacking vital brain cells?' I suggested.

Bert threw water at me. So I dunked him.

'Excuse US,' snapped Arabella, 'but would you mind explaining yourselves? As you keep reminding us, two of us here aren't pirates.'

Bert and I turned to Arabella and George. We both grinned.

You see, a pirate does not sleep like a normal person. Normal people go to bed in the evening then sleep soundly till morning before eating a bowl of cornflakes. All very nice and sensible.

But we pirates aren't sensible. We stay up late playing card games and telling rude jokes and counting treasure. And sometimes – quite often actually – we stay awake all night. This is because we have to keep watch for other ships. But it's also because we want to have a good time. We're party animals.

But the only way we can stay up all night is by having a nap in the afternoon. All pirates have an afternoon nap, even mums and dads. We just pass out on the deck or in a hammock. We call it our crashout. During a crashout we sleep so deeply hardly anything disturbs us.

I smiled at Arabella. 'We won't have to wait out all night. My guess is that Captain Guillemot is going to need his afternoon crashout VERY soon. Remember? He told us he needed his beauty sleep. After all this partying, he'll be exhausted. We just have to wait until he's flat out. Then we can go in and rescue Maud.'

We pulled ourselves up on to the rocks and waited. It was our only hope.

We waited for a long time. So long that Bert and I started to fall asleep ourselves – after all, we need our crashouts as much as the next pirate.

I woke up when I fell into the water.

'Bert!' I said, spitting out a small fish and shaking my brother awake. 'Listen!'

'Rollock off,' said Bert grumpily. 'I'm sleepy.'

'I can't hear anything,' said Arabella. 'And unlike you two, I've been awake all this time.'

'I can't hear anything, either,' I said. I started to get excited. 'Which means . . .'

Bert rubbed his eyes and grinned.

'They've fallen asleep!' he said.

'Exactly,' I said, grabbing our coil of rope and getting ready to swim again. 'It's time to rescue our sister.'

CHAPTER
13

The water in the cave was icy cold and black. Small fish bit my toes and cold drips fell from the ceiling on to my nose. I couldn't see more than a few metres in front of me.

It was nasty.

None of us said anything for a few minutes. We were too busy concentrating on swimming.

Arabella kept saying, 'Hmmm'. She was either very scared or very good at concentrating. I think maybe it was both, although she had one of those faces that didn't look scared. Not like our family.

We were either really happy or really sad or really cross or really friendly. But Arabella and George – their faces were just one thing, all the time. Not like pirates at all. Arabella never took her eyes off the surface of the water, not for a minute. Bert and I kept getting distracted by having a little fight. Or by finding a crab claw and putting it down each other's T-shirt. Or dangling wet pieces of seaweed over each other's heads. But Arabella just kept on going. She led us carefully under stalactites and through a pool full of weeds. She didn't once make a sound, and

this is actually just what you want from the person in front. You need them to be steady.

We paused on another rocky ledge.

'Maud had better be in here,' Bert grumbled.

'Don't worry,' Arabella said. 'We'll find her. George is very good at finding things, aren't you, George? Hide-and-seek is one of his best things – after knitting. Everybody is good at something. That's what Mrs Richie says. Mrs Richie is our favourite teacher, isn't she, George?'

George concentrated on treading water.

I coughed to hide a laugh. Imagine having a favourite teacher. We hate school and we hate teachers. All of them. If there was a queue of people waiting to walk the plank, I'd put all the teachers right at the front and cheer as they fell in the water.

We started swimming again.

Bert looked at Arabella. 'If everyone's good at something, what are you so good at then?' he spluttered.

'Well,' said Arabella, breaststroking to keep up with Bert and not noticing his sarcasm. 'I'm an ideas lady. I decide what the best thing to do is and then I work out how to do it. It's amazing how few people can do this. I might run the country one day. Dad says he wouldn't be at all surprised.'

Arabella was one of the most annoying non-pirates I had ever met. And nearly all of them annoyed me so this was saying something. She was boastful too, like Bert. But the truth was, I could see her as prime minister. I mean look at her. She was only ten and she knew how to steer a boat across a stormy sea. She knew all about the history of square-rigger boats. She knew how to track a bloodthirsty famous pirate across a desert island. She understood the geology of caves, for parrot's sake. She was a bit of a sea dog.

Perhaps she really would help us rescue our sister.

Bert and I looked at each other. I could tell exactly what Bert was thinking. *What am I good at then?*

I put him out of his misery. 'You're really, really good at saying stupid things,' I said.

Bert scowled and pushed me. He pushed me so hard, I scudded straight past Arabella and before I could say, 'You're the worst brother in the world!' . . . I bumped into something very hard.

'What is it?' asked Arabella. 'Is something in the way?'

Bert snorted. I gave him a look.

'Everyone keep their voices down,' I hissed. 'Now!'

Arabella squinted. 'Oh,' she said.

'Yes,' I whispered.

The thing I had bumped into was no rock. It was the back end of a boat, A.K.A. a stern. Bert calls the stern the ship's bum. Maud calls it the dragon's bot because she thinks pirate ships are shaped like dragons. And this? This was definitely a dragon's bot.

Arabella shrugged. 'That's a stern,' she said. 'A big stern.'

'Yes, we KNOW it's a stern,' Bert said witheringly. 'The question is, whose stern is it?'

'Well,' whispered Arabella, 'putting a few things together I wouldn't have thought it was very difficult to work that one out. This must be Captain Guillemot's ship. So the question actually is, what do we do now?'

Hanging over the back of the ship's stern was a

rope ladder. Bert grabbed it and started to climb up.

'Bert!' I hissed. 'Wait! Remember what's at the top.'

'I don't care,' Bert muttered. 'I'm not staying in this creepy water one moment longer. My legs are being bitten by slimy fish and my fingers have gone all wrinkly. Plus,' he continued, 'our little sister is up there – and I'm not going to let anything happen to her.'

Bert carried on climbing. I told you he never listens.

Arabella and I pulled a face at each other.

'Maybe if we creep up really slowly,' I whispered, 'we can just peer over the top and see what's happening. After all, Bert's right, we can't give up on Maud. I really hope she's OK.'

Arabella shrugged again. 'She's certainly the most independent three-year-old I've ever come across. I wouldn't want to cross *her* on a dark night. And I wouldn't want to cross her in a dark cave.'

I chuckled. 'You really wouldn't want to, I can tell you,' I said proudly. 'Especially if she's having her afternoon crashout. There's nothing that makes her crosser than being woken up. Even Mum gets a bit scared of her in the mornings when we have to lift her out of her washing-up bowl bed. She's a terror.'

'Is she now?' muttered Arabella grimly. Personally, I couldn't decide which of them – Arabella or Maud – was worse. They both had the same habit of knowing exactly what they were doing. And sticking to it.

Arabella, George and I set off up the rope ladder after Bert, one rung at a time.

CHAPTER

14

Have you ever heard a pirate snoring? I bet you haven't. You'd remember if you had.

All pirates snore. Mum is the worst. Dad says she sounds like a hibernating bear. He has to steal earplugs from the supermarket. He tries to keep them a secret but Mum always finds out. She finds out about everything. Then she just laughs and carries on snoring.

Anyway, my point is – we pirates are used to snoring.

So the moment Arabella and I stepped off the

rope ladder and heard the roars, I knew EXACTLY what it was. Unlike Arabella, who looked terrified.

'What's that awful noise?!' she gasped.

'That,' I whispered, 'is music to my ears. That is the noise of sleeping pirates. And I've been at sea long enough to know that sleeping pirates are way easier to deal with than wide-awake pirates.'

The loud rumbling noise echoed around the ship, ricocheting off the cave walls. And it was followed by little grumbly splutters and drools.

'ZZz z zzzzz'

Arabella opened her mouth as if to say something, then stopped.

Captain Guillemot was sprawled on the deck in front of us. His mouth was wide open. We could see right in. Bits of food were stuck between his gold teeth. His tonsils were purple and they wobbled as he breathed.

He looked much bigger close up.

He looked even more scary.

We tiptoed over him and his crew.

'ZZZZZZZZ'

'Bert?' I whispered. 'Where are you?'

Bert leaped out suddenly from under a folded-up sail.

'I got here first,' he whispered triumphantly. 'I beat you!'

'Only cos you were too stupid to wait,' I told him.

'They don't look so bad, do they?' said Arabella, examining the pirates.

'That's because they're asleep,' Bert told her furiously.

'They're certainly very noisy,' agreed Arabella.

'But where's Maud?' I hissed. 'What have they done with her?'

'Maud?' Bert called out as loud as he could without breaking out of his whisper.

'Maud?' I said in my quietest loud voice.

For a few moments, all we heard was snoring. Until, all of a sudden, the cave began to echo with the sound of a loud, three-year-old's giggle.

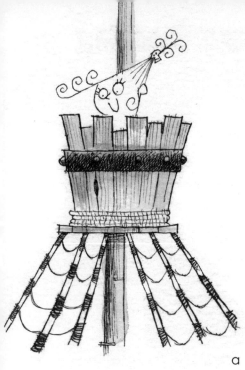

'Can't catch me!' cackled Maud.

I spun round and looked up. There, right up in the crow's nest of Captain Guillemot's pirate ship, was our very blond, very smiley baby sister. For a few seconds I had to stop myself from leaping up and down on the spot and singing in my loudest voice. I was so happy that Maud was still alive.

'Maud!' I whispered. 'Are you OK?'

Maud gave me the thumbs up. I gave her a wave. But then I looked at her more closely and gulped. There was nothing around her neck.

'Maud!' I hissed. 'Where's the Blighty Bling?'

Maud crossed her arms over her chest. 'The horridish pirate stoled it,' she said. 'So I screamed my best scream and he tried to squish me with his anchor.

So I climbed up here and he had a crashout.' Maud pointed at Captain Guillemot. 'He's a bad man.'

'Maud,' I said. 'Well done. He's a very bad man. But Maud, where did he put the Blighty Bling?'

Captain Guillemot twitched and stirred. We held our breath and waited. Then he gave a long loud snore and settled back down to sleep.

'Maud,' I hissed up to the crow's nest. 'Maud, listen to me.'

Maud put her head to one side.

'We need to get that Blighty Bling right now and then we need to go back home to Mum and Dad. Maud! I'll get you a super-sized bag of strawberry sherbets for supper tonight if you tell me where he put the Blighty Bling. You want to get home for those, don't you?'

Maud sucked in her cheeks. She looked from me, to Bert, to Arabella, to George. She put on her cutest, least trustworthy face. 'Maud is very, very tired,' she said, putting her thumb in her mouth. 'Maud needs to crashout. Night night, Vic, night night, Bert, night night, smarty girl, night night, funny big boy. See you later.'

Maud curled up in a neat ball and fell fast asleep.
George laughed. He'd never done that before.

'Blimey,' said Arabella. 'I thought it was meant to
be hard to get babies to go to sleep.'

I shrugged. 'I told you pirates need their crashouts.
Maud is nasty without hers. The important thing now
is NOT to wake her up, or she won't be happy at all.'

'So what are we meant to do, just wait for her to
wake while we're surrounded by all these villains?'
Arabella waved her arms wildly at the sleeping pirates.

I felt a wash of despair. Here we were standing on
a pirate ship belonging to our old arch-enemy. Who
(for the record) was asleep and snoring with his entire
crew right next to our feet. Our sister was also fast
asleep right up in the crow's nest. She had lost the
Blighty Bling and she wouldn't tell us where Captain
Guillemot had hidden it. We had no captain, no map.
And our pet parrot was missing, presumed dead.

Things did not look good.

But one thing was certain. The Blighty Bling
would have to wait. Getting Maud back was more
important.

131

'Right,' I told the others. 'One thing we do have is rope,' I pulled out the coil of rope that was strapped to my back. 'We may as well use it to tie up this lot.'

I started to unravel the rope.

'Then, when they wake up,' I continued, 'they won't be able to capture us – or at least not straight away.'

It wasn't the best plan in the world but we didn't have a better one.

Tying up fully grown, sleeping pirates is trickier than it looks. The rope was wet and heavy and the pirates' arms and legs were awkward to lift. Plus, we were terrified of waking them up. Each time one of them spluttered or moved, we had to stop and hold our breath. It took us nearly an hour to tie up Beefster, Bones and Cath and we hadn't even started on Guillemot.

It was just occurring to me that we probably should have tied up the captain first when I noticed we had another problem. We had run out of rope.

'We can't have,' whispered Arabella, who was busy wiping sweat from George's head.

'Well, we have,' I replied gloomily.

Arabella stood up and scanned the boat. 'There must be lots more rope on a ship this size. We just need to look for it.'

We headed off.

I made for the bow of the ship (which, by the way, is the name for the front) and had a rummage. I was hoping there might be a spare piece of rope hanging near the anchor. This is common on most boats.

It was so dark I had to squint to get a proper look. I peered over *The Raven*'s bow. But what I actually saw made me belch out loud. I always belch when something surprises me and I was proper surprised right now. No, surprised is the wrong word. I was blimmin' flabbergasted.

CHAPTER

15

At first I thought it was a ghost ship.

But then I pinched myself six and a half times and looked again.

There, in front of me, tied up to the walls of this horrible dark cave, was our very own family pirate ship, *Sixpoint Sally*.

The one we thought had sunk to the bottom of the sea a year ago.

I heard a loud burp beside me. It was Bert.

Bert paused and grabbed my hand. Bert never grabs my hand so I couldn't help jumping in surprise.

'That can't be her,' he whispered. 'Mum and Dad sank her and lost (nearly) all our treasure. That's what you told me.'

'That's what *they* told me,' I hissed. My mouth had gone very dry. For some reason, seeing our old pirate ship again wasn't making me leap up and down on the spot with excitement. It had the opposite effect. I felt all wobbly as though I might fall asleep. I hadn't realised how much I'd missed her this past year. I hadn't realised how important it was to have a place where we belonged. Living in a caravan just isn't right for scurvy sea dogs like us.

But Bert was right. She was meant to be lying at the bottom of the ocean – at least that's what Mum and Dad had told us.

'She looks good,' Bert said proudly. 'She looks fine.'

I nodded. *Sixpoint Sally* looked tip-top.

'She didn't sink.'

'Nope.'

'Hasn't got a scratch on her.'

'Hmmm.'

It didn't make sense. If Mum and Dad hadn't sunk our pirate ship, why did they say they had?

I thought back to the times I'd asked them about the shipwreck. There was obviously something they weren't telling us.

'Whatever happened,' I told Bert, 'we need to get her back.'

'Oh well,' said Bert sarcastically, 'if that's all we've got to do, we're laughing. I mean it's so incredibly simple. Just a small matter of taking down an entire adult pirate crew, unearthing the Blighty Bling, sailing *Sixpoint Sally* past *The Raven*, finding our way out of the cave, navigating the Hammerhead Rocks and out into the open seas. Then all we need to do is make our way home and return the Blighty Bling to its box before Mum and Dad get home. Should be a piece of cake. And that,' he went on, gathering momentum and puffing out his chest, 'that's all after we've got round the teeny tiny incy squincy problem of waking up a three-year-old who doesn't like to be woken up.'

Bert looked at me mockingly. 'Plus,' he continued,

'have you seen how *Sally* is tied up? Look at those knots. We'll never undo them, they're stump knots.'

I nodded. For once in his life Bert was right. *Sixpoint Sally* was covered in a maze of ropes, tied in complex knots and weird patterns. All pirates have their own secret knotting code, it's a bit like a special language. You lot have things like car alarms but these are no good to us pirates – no one would hear them. Complicated knots are way more effective and Captain Guillemot is famous for using the most complicated of all – stump knots.

I felt horrible. Here we were, so close to reclaiming our family ship, and we couldn't do anything.

George had been listening in silence. But he didn't say anything, either. He just hopped aboard our old family ship and started snooping around as if he was looking for something. He didn't even ask our permission.

'Hey,' I hissed. 'What do you think you're looking for? That's McScurvy private property, that is. Everything on that boat belongs to us, not you.'

I was about to give him a good talking-to.

But then Arabella called out to us from the stern of *The Raven*.

'Come quickly!' she said. 'They're starting to wake up.'

We raced back to the ship's bridge. Arabella was right. The pirates had stopped snoring and were beginning to twitch, and Captain Guillemot still wasn't tied up.

'Right!' I said. 'We haven't got long. One of us has got to climb the mast and get Maud down from the crow's nest before they wake.'

I told Bert to start climbing. He told me off for being bossy. We were still arguing about who should climb the mast when we noticed Arabella was already halfway up. We couldn't let a non-pirate girl rescue our sister for us. So we set off behind her.

Climbing a mast is easier than climbing trees because there are more footholds. But what makes things difficult is the constant rocking of the boat in the water. What's more, *The Raven*'s mast was harder to climb than most because it was made of polished mahogany. In other words we kept

slipping and sliding.

Arabella was very slow and we soon caught up with her. But it's very difficult to overtake somebody on a mast so for quite a few minutes all we could do was stare at her bottom.

I crossed my fingers she wouldn't fart.

But actually a fart would have been OK because what happened was way worse.

CHAPTER
16

Now I'm guessing you don't know what a Timber Terror is. I'll explain.

Most pirates have had a Timber Terror once in their life. Even our mum and dad have had one. But just because they're a common occurrence doesn't stop them from being very, very scary.

At first a Timber Terror makes you feel dizzy. Then you lose all the feeling in your legs and are stuck to the spot. Then you go hot in the face and cold in the stomach. Then you think you are going to die.

We pirates know that the best way to avoid a

Timber Terror is to not look down. Because when you're at the top of a mast, it always looks a lot further than it really is.

If you look down from the top of the mast, you're pretty much guaranteed to have a Timber Terror.

Halfway up that mast, Arabella made the mistake of looking down. And she had the skipper of all Timber Terrors.

First of all she started to shake.

Then she started to cry.

Then she started to wimper and wail.

She was well and truly stuck. There was no way she could climb back down on her own – let alone up.

Meanwhile, down on deck, I could see that the tied-up sleeping pirates were twitching like crazy. And George was nowhere to be seen. He was still snooping around our boat.

'I'll help Arabella back down, you go after Maud,' I told Bert. 'You're the best climber.'

I waited for Bert to start gloating because I'd paid him a compliment but to my surprise he didn't.

He just pulled himself up that mast like a monkey, picking his way carefully past Arabella as if she wasn't even in his way.

Sometimes, just sometimes, Bert is OK.

Arabella, on the other hand, was definitely NOT OK.

Dad once rescued me from a Timber Terror so I tried to remember everything he had said and done.

I told Arabella to look straight ahead, then I climbed down ahead of her, putting her feet on to each foothold as we came to it, guiding her hands to each handhold. It wasn't easy because Arabella kept grabbing my hair and screaming. And every time she looked down, she had a new bout of shakes.

It felt like hours but it was probably only about three minutes. That's the thing about Timber Terrors, they seem to last for ever but as soon as you reach the ground you feel fine again. It's like seasickness. It's like magic.

Once Arabella was herself again, I looked up to see how Bert was getting on. He'd reached the crow's nest and was stretching out his hands to get Maud.

'Don't wake her,' I called up at him. But I couldn't shout because I didn't want to wake the pirates.

Bert didn't hear.

He grinned down at us, waving his arms and behaving like a complete idiot.

I could tell he was chuffed that he was the one who had got to rescue Maud rather than me. He was rubbing it in. He was going to go on and on about this for years.

I scowled at him but he kept on waving.

'Don't wake her!'

I shouted more loudly.

CHAPTER 17

Bert woke Maud.

And Maud did what she always does when someone wakes her.

Maud SCREAMED.

She screamed so loudly that our eyes started to water.

She screamed so loudly that the sails started to flap.

She screamed so loudly that Captain Guillemot and his crew woke up.

Arabella and I hid behind a sail bag and watched them.

They were not a pretty sight.

No one looks – or smells – their best when they are woken up. But pirates are even worse. Captain Guillemot looked HORRIBLE. His sunburnt face was all puffed up, especially around his piggy eyes. Dark blue veins ran across his nose and angry frown lines ran down the middle of his forehead. He had sweaty patches under the arms of his waistcoat. His cheeks were spotty and stubbly. He stank of old fish and stale blood.

He did not like Maud's screaming.

'Someone shut that kid up!' he roared.

The other pirates tried to stand up but they couldn't because their hands and feet were tied. They wriggled around like three big babies.

Maud's screams got louder.

The pirates buried their heads into the deck.

'STOP!' cried Beefster.

'Make that baby STOP!'

Arabella and I crouched down as far as we could. It wouldn't be long before they broke free of the knots we'd tied. Then they'd be looking for revenge. I imagined Guillemot biting off my fingers and toes and feeding them to his pet piranhas (after all, this is what happened to Uncle Ray). I imagined him making Arabella and George walk the plank. I imagined him popping Bert and Maud in buckets and tossing them far out to sea.

I opened my eyes a crack. But to my surprise, Captain Guillemot was not biting off our fingers and his crew were not breaking free of our knots.

They were not getting ready to lock us in the torture chamber.

They were not brandishing cutlasses. No.

They looked terrified.

'Ha!' whispered Arabella. 'Those brutes clearly can't bear the sound of a baby crying. So often the case with bullies. I think it's time we took advantage.'

I saw what she meant. Maud's screaming had given us a chance.

One good thing about living with a sister who

screams a lot is . . . you get used to it.

I climbed out from behind the sail bag and stood up tall.

'OOOH AAAGHGHGHGHGH!'

I said to Captain Guillemot. I sounded much braver than I felt.

'NOT YOU LOT AGAIN!' roared Captain Guillemot. 'You'd better make that sister of yours shut up. Or you'll all be sorry.'

The fat pirate called Beefster looked like he might cry. The other two tried to cover their ears but because their hands were tied they could only cover one ear at a time. They looked miserable.

'**Shut her up,**' they begged.

'Tape up her mouth.'

'Throw her overboard.'

'MAKE that BABY STOP.'

Arabella tutted. 'Honestly,' she said, 'fancy big brave baddies like you making such a fuss about a tired baby. You should be ashamed of yourselves.'

'GET. HER. OUT. OF. HERE!' roared Guillemot.

'All in good time,' I said. My voice sounded very wobbly in the echoey cave. 'But first we want to take back something that belongs to us.'

I looked Guillemot straight in the eye and tried not to show him how scared I felt.

'If you let us have *Sixpoint Sally* back,' I said,

154

'we'll tell Maud to stop.'

Captain Guillemot grimaced and pushed his hands further over his ears.

'No chance,' he said, wincing. 'That ship is mine.'

'That ship,' I replied, 'is OURS. She's McScurvy property.'

Captain Guillemot gave a nasty laugh. 'Correction, my little firecracker,' he said. 'She WAS McScurvy property but she isn't any more. I won her fair and square. Your dad lost her to me in a game of cards. He didn't have enough money to pay me and he wouldn't give me the Blighty Bling. So I took your ship instead.'

I gasped.

'Liar!' I said. '*Sixpoint Sally* sank on the Hammerhead Rocks. Everyone knows that.'

'Wrong again!' said Guillemot, clamping his hands over his ears. 'That's what your parents told you because they didn't want you to know the truth – that they squandered your birthright over a game of pontoon.'

I swallowed. Could this be true? Had our

parents lied to us? I cast my mind back to a year ago and went over what Mum and Dad had said. But the weird thing was, I couldn't remember them mentioning anything about a shipwreck. All they'd said was that they'd LOST *Sixpoint Sally* somewhere on the rocks that surround Puffin Island. It was me who decided she must have sunk. I'd jumped to the wrong conclusion.

I didn't know whether to feel cross with myself for getting the wrong end of the stick or pleased that Mum and Dad hadn't lied to us. But mainly I just felt glad that *Sixpoint Sally* wasn't lying at the bottom of the sea.

Guillemot ground his gold teeth.

'I WON'T give you back your tatty old rust bucket of a ship,' he said nastily. 'So there.'

He glanced at Maud.

'Louder, Maudie!' I shouted up the mast. 'Scream as loud as you can.'

Up on the crow's nest Bert was busy arranging Maud over his shoulders. He started to climb back down the mast.

He grinned and waved at us all.

'Stop waving, you idiot!' I shouted at him. 'You'll drop her.'

But Bert didn't hear. He just waved again.

'NOOOOOOOOO!'

wailed Bert, losing his grip on Maud's ankles.

'Waaaaaghghghgghh!'

screamed Maud, falling head first towards us.

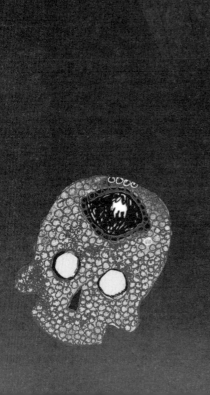

CHAPTER

18

The only thing to do when your little sister is about to die is to be the hero of the hour.

In the few seconds I had to think, the very worst scenario dawned on me. Maud was going to smash her head on the deck of the ship and she was going to die.

I tried. I really tried.

But catching has never been my strong point. Mum calls me butterfingers. I like to think I'm more of a kicker.

I leaped to the bottom of the mast. I looked up

at Maud's pink face hurtling towards me. I closed my eyes and I stretched out my arms, hoping to catch her but . . .

. . . I missed.

I opened my eyes slowly, expecting to see Maud sprawled and bloody on the deck. But what I saw instead was . . .

. . . a grubby white blanket.

It was stretched out between Arabella and George like a safety net and it looked ever so slightly familiar. I took a closer look.

It was Maud's nuggy!

And, sitting in the middle of the nuggy, smiling her rotten-tooth grin, was Maud.

'George knew how much Maud wanted her nuggy so he went to look for it in your old pirate ship,' Arabella explained. 'He loves finding things, but even he didn't know it would end up saving her life.' She paused and patted George on the shoulder. Then she grinned at me. 'We both play cricket for the county.'

I could have hugged them.

'Nuggy,' said Maud happily, jumping off her blanket and putting it straight in her mouth. 'Nuggy, nuggy, nuggy,' she said, sucking it.

Then she leaped into George's arms and gave him a sloppy kiss.

George went bright red.

Bert jumped down from the mast.

'You shouldn't have dropped her,' I told him.

'You shouldn't have missed.'

We almost had a fight about that but then we noticed Guillemot.

Maud was so happy to have her nuggy back she refused to start screaming again, no matter how much we begged her to. Which meant our old arch-enemy was back in action.

'Relax,' he told his tied-up crew. 'It's just the McScurvy brats. Nothing to worry about. Have you enjoyed your little trip to the deep dark cave? Have you seen all the pretty stalactites and stalagmites?'

'As a matter of fact,' said Arabella. 'I learned all about caves in Year One. We saw stalagmites and everything back then. We're not interested in caves any more, not one bit, we're interested in taking back what is ours.'

Captain Guillemot laughed and laughed and laughed until tears streamed down his red stubbly face.

'Oh my days,' he said, still laughing. 'You're hilarious. Absolutely killing! Take back what's yours indeed? And what might that be, my little ginger nut?'

Arabella scowled. 'Jolly well don't call me ginger nut,' she told Captain Guillemot crossly.

Captain Guillemot laughed even more loudly.

'I jolly well will!' he said.

Bert pointed his cutlass at Captain Guillemot.

'You can laugh all you like,' he said. 'But we're taking our sister home and you're going to give us the Blighty Bling and we're taking our ship back too.'

Captain Guillemot nearly fell over.

Now he broke into a loud guffaw.

'HA HA HA HA!' he cackled, not looking at all worried. 'Hecky thump,' he said to his crew, wiping tears of laughter out of his eyes. 'It's the darstardly McScurvys. I'm so scared!' He giggled. 'I'm so worried they'll hurt me. I'm so frightened they'll figure out how to undo those stump knots. Oh my giddy aunt.'

Beefster, Bones and Cath collapsed into giggles.

Captain Guillemot still hadn't got round to untying them. He was too busy checking on his reflection in his pocket mirror and redoing his hair.

He was right though. We didn't have a hope of beating him and his crew. And even if we did, we'd never be able to undo the stump knots on *Sixpoint Sally*.

We were well and truly stuck.

'I can't decide,' said Guillemot, looking up from his reflection and pouting at us instead, 'whether to make you walk the plank straight away or torture you for hours. Which would be more fun?'

Cath snorted.

'We could keep them as pets?' she suggested.

Beefster guffawed.

'Or use 'em for shark bait. Sharks love children.'

Bones got the giggles. 'We could cook them in a big pot and watch them turn pink,' he said nastily.

I closed my eyes.

I couldn't help thinking of Mum and Dad arriving back at our caravan and finding us missing.

If only I hadn't picked up the Blighty Bling this

morning. This was all my fault.

I looked at Bert. I looked at Arabella. I looked at George and Maud. I looked at our two slightly rusty cutlasses.

I gulped.

'**Fight!**' I shouted. '**Fight for your LIVES!**'

CHAPTER 19

Swipe!

I knocked Captain Guillemot's cutlass out of his hand. It fell to the floor with a clank.

'Rapscallion!' he shouted. 'I need that.'

He tried to pick up his cutlass but Arabella whacked him on the bottom. Her face was bright pink and her mouth was all wiggly. She looked like Dad does when he steers into something. She looked flustered.

'Ow!' roared Guillemot, clutching his backside.

Arabella leaned forward and grabbed his cutlass.

She pointed it at him.

'That's against the rules!' yelled Guillemot. 'Pirates don't steal other pirates' cutlasses.'

'Irrelevant,' said Arabella, swooshing the cutlass in front of his face. 'I'm not a real pirate so I don't give two sherbets about your silly rules. Anyway, you shouldn't pick fights with people smaller than you!'

Arabella's hand was shaking. I could tell she was scared. But this wasn't necessarily bad. Mum says being scared is a sign of bravery. She says people who don't get scared are stupid, not brave. She says any old pirate can be stupid and that's a fact. Arabella was not any old pirate.

Bert and I stood either side of her. We pointed our cutlasses at Captain Guillemot.

Captain Guillemot turned to his crew.

'Do something, horseflies,' he shouted. 'Get off your backsides and HELP ME.'

But they were still tied up. All they could do was shout.

Arabella took a deep breath and pointed

Captain Guillemot's sword at his belly. It made a small dent in his waistcoat.

Captain Guillemot exploded.

'How DARE you?! That's a designer waistcoat. It's French couture. It cost me a hundred gold coins and an antique pearl necklace. It makes me look *sick*. If you damage it, I'll chew you into tiny pieces!'

Arabella pushed her cutlass in a bit further. Her hand shook.

'If you don't want me to damage your precious waistcoat,' she said bravely, 'you'll have to let us go. George and I need to be back in time for supper or our parents will call the police.'

Captain Guillemot laughed so much his whole body shook. He laughed so much he got the hiccups.

For a moment I thought he might let us go after all.

I was wrong.

Crack!

With one smooth pincer movement, Captain Guillemot kick-boxed Arabella to the ground and winded her. Then he grabbed his cutlass back.

'Take that, ginger nut,' he shouted, laughing nastily.

Then he turned to me and Bert.

Flecks of saliva glistened on his lips. I could see pink gums pulsing between his gold teeth. His mouth got closer and closer to my nose. He was going to bite it off.

Swipe!

Bert went for Guillemot's belly. But Guillemot dodged it easily. Then he tripped Bert up, flipped him to the ground and put a foot on top of his head.

Bert's cutlass flew to the other side of the deck.

Swish!

I aimed my cutlass at the top of Guillemot's head but he swerved just in time. Then he picked me up in one hand and threw me on top of Bert.

My cutlass flew off in the opposite direction.

Arabella staggered to her feet but Guillemot swung his cutlass at her head. She put her hands over her face and screamed.

I saw two ginger locks floating in slow motion through the air.

George couldn't help because he was carrying Maud. But even if his arms had been free I knew there was nothing he could do. Captain Guillemot was bigger and stronger than all of us put together and he was way more skillful too. He leaned over us and laughed.

'I think I'll start with the fingers,' he said, salivating.

I closed my eyes. I felt drops of his spit landing on my forehead. Any minute now, those gold teeth would be biting into me. I waited to hear the horrible crunch of bones and flesh. Now it was about to happen, I just wanted it to be over with quickly.

But, instead, I heard something else. Something familiar.

It was a flapping sound.

I listened again just to make sure I hadn't mistaken it for a sail or a flag. But, no, this was a gentle, rhythmic flap. It was the sound of a bird, a bird I knew well.

I opened my eyes.

Hovering, high up in the darkness of the cave, was our very wet and very cross-looking parrot.

'Pedro!' I whispered.

He hadn't drowned after all.

Pedro cackled. He circled Captain Guillemot. He started to squawk.

'Take this!' he said.

Out of Pedro's bottom came a very large . . . SPLAT!

A dollop of brown and white parrot poo landed right in the middle of Captain Guillemot's expensive waistcoat.

SPLAT, SPLAT, SPLAT!

'STOP IT!' screamed Captain Guillemot in horror. 'This waistcoat is dry-clean only.'

He pulled his bandana off his head and started to dab at the splats of bird poo. For a moment, he forgot about biting off our fingers.

'Pedro!' I murmured under my breath. 'You're a genius. You're a lifesaver. You're ALIVE!'

Pedro squawked again. 'Clever parrot, clever parrot!' he said.

We all started to giggle.

This made Captain Guillemot angrier than ever. Remember, he hates people laughing at him.

'STOP IT!' he yelled. 'I am Captain Guillemot the Third. I am the most feared and stylish pirate on the whole entire planet. I will NOT be laughed at by a bunch of brats.'

The more we tried to stop, the more we laughed.

We couldn't help it.

Pedro hovered above, squawking loudly.

'Go away!' snapped Captain Guillemot. 'Just go away, you feathery frip! You've ruined my best waistcoat.'

Captain Guillemot took it off and smoothed it out on deck to inspect the damage.

'Quick,' hissed Arabella. 'Get up while he's not looking.'

We got up.

'Right,' whispered Arabella. 'Now line up behind him and get ready to push.'

We did what she said.

'Ready?' said Arabella.

We nodded.

Then we shoved Captain Guillemot as hard as we could.

His feet slipped.

He staggered forward.

He fell head first over the side.

SPLASH!

'Run!' I told the others. 'Run to *Sixpoint Sally*.'

We turned to go. But then I spotted Maud. She had wriggled out of George's arms and was now racing to the edge of the deck.

'Maud!' I said, trying to sound like Mum. 'Come. Here. Right. Now!'

Maud ignored me and picked up Guillemot's waistcoat.

'Maud!' I shouted. 'Leave that. We don't need it!'

Maud ignored me again. She put the waistcoat over her shoulders. She stood at the edge of the deck so Captain Guillemot could see her, and posed as if someone was taking a picture of her.

Guillemot swam frantically towards the ladder that hung over the side of his boat.

'Get it off her!' he shouted from the water below. 'That's mine!'

Captain Guillemot sounded a lot more like Mum than I did. But it didn't make any difference. Maud ignored him too.

'Maud!' I shouted. 'For once in your life, listen to me!'

Maud looked at me and grinned. She turned away from Guillemot and sauntered towards us. She didn't even rush.

Guillemot shouted again.

'STOP THAT BABY!' he bellowed.

Out of the corner of my eye I saw him getting closer to his boat.

'Maud!' I screamed. 'Hurry!'

But Maud was still in no rush. She was fiddling around with the waistcoat.

Beefster grabbed at Maud with the tips of his fingers. He pinched the waistcoat between his thumb and forefinger and started to pull.

Maud tried to slap him away.

Bert and I raced forward.

I grabbed one of Maud's feet. Bert grabbed the other.

We pulled.

But, even with his hands tied up, Beefster was way stronger than us.

The palms of my hands got wet with sweat. Maud was slipping away.

'Heave!' I told Bert. 'Heave ho!'

We pulled as hard as we could.

Rip! Guillemot's waistcoat started to tear.

'Yes!' shouted Bert.

'No!' shouted Guillemot.

'FART!' shouted Maud, flying out

of the torn waistcoat and landing at our feet.

But we didn't have time to cheer.

Guillemot had nearly reached the ladder.

I lifted Maud on to my back. I shouted to the others.

And we all jumped at the same time.

CHAPTER
20

For a moment it felt great to be back on board *Sixpoint Sally*.

The soles of my bare feet seemed to know every scratch and nick of our ship's scrubbed wooden deck. Even her smell – of salty sails and sugary cups of tea – was exactly as I remembered. She was like an old friend. She was safe. She was our home.

But as drips of condensation fell from the roof of the cave into the inky black water below, I looked at the complicated ropes that secured *Sixpoint Sally* to the walls and knew that we weren't safe at all.

We had no idea how to undo the stump knots.

I sighed and looked at Bert. He sighed back at me. We knew what this meant. We'd come so close to reclaiming our family ship. We'd come so close to escaping and now . . .

. . . now we were completely and utterly stuck.

Any minute now Captain Guillemot would climb back up on to his ship. Then he'd release his crew and they'd recapture us in no time.

There was no way a dangerous pirate like Guillemot was going to let the McScurvy children and their non-pirate pals get the better of him a second time.

Pedro squawked. He always squawks when something bad is about to happen.

'Shut up, Pedro!' said Bert. 'We're trying to think.'

But thinking didn't help.

I put my head in my hands. For a moment everything went quiet. I couldn't hear Pedro squawking. I couldn't hear Bert muttering. I couldn't even hear my own breath.

But I could hear a loud shriek.

'Bravo, George!' said Arabella.

I looked up.

Arabella was grinning.

Why was she looking so chirpy? Didn't she know what danger we were all in?

I was about to tell her to wipe the smile off her face when I noticed what she was looking at.

George was bustling about on deck. His head was down and his hands were moving fast. George was untying the stump knots.

'I told you!' said Arabella proudly. 'I told you that George absolutely LOVES knitting. And anyone who's good at knitting is used to untying knots. Granny says George is even better at untangling than she is.'

I believed her.

If there was an Olympic medal for untying knots, I reckon George would have won it. He was even quicker than Mum and Dad and they'd studied knots at pirate university. They had years of practice.

George was just untying the last stump knot when

Pedro squawked again.

'Look out!' he said. 'Look out!'

We glanced up.

Over on *The Raven*, Captain Guillemot was back on board. He was soaking wet and he looked crosser than ever. I could see his gold teeth glinting in the darkness.

He was using them to bite through the ropes that tied up his crew.

'Get the oars,' I told Bert. 'Hoist the sails. GET THIS SHIP SHIPSHAPE.'

I placed my hand against the cold wet wall of the cave and pushed as hard as I could. I felt *Sally* float towards the main channel of water. Then I raced back to the bridge and grabbed the ship's wheel.

We were off.

Overtaking *The Raven* took a long time because there was no wind inside the cave to fill our sails. We could only drift along gently with the current. To make things trickier, Captain Guillemot and his crew kept throwing things at us. We had to duck and swerve to avoid flying scrubbing brushes and old fish hooks.

But once we'd got past them, the current became stronger and we sped up.

Pedro led the way and I steered while Arabella and Bert pushed their hands against the sides of the cave to help push *Sally* forward. George played peekaboo with Maud.

As we moved further and further towards sunlight I began to cheer up.

We'd saved our sister. We'd (nearly) escaped from Captain Guillemot.

Not many pirate kids could say that.

Not many grown-up pirates could say that, either.

But no matter how hard I tried, I couldn't enjoy myself. I was still thinking about the Blighty Bling.

It was the most famous jewel in pirate history. It was the most important thing our family had ever owned. It was the one thing Mum and Dad treasured more than anything else.

And we'd lost it.

We reached the calm saltwater pool we'd swum into earlier and slowed *Sally* to a halt. We all knew that the Hammerhead Rocks were out there somewhere, lurking under the water.

'Well, come on,' said Arabella. 'Find the right map, find out where the rocks are hidden, and plot the right course out. Where's your chart table?'

Bert and I rolled our eyes.

Anyone knows that decent pirates don't plot their routes on charts. They use the sun and the wind and deep pirate knowledge.

Dad calls it instinct.

Mum says it depends on how many instincts he's drunk.

But, anyway, they manage.

We, on the other hand, were not managing. The swell of the tide was pulling *Sixpoint Sally* all over the place. My arms ached and there were rocks everywhere.

Bert cleared his throat. 'We don't have a chart table. We don't have charts. We're pirates, remember. The only maps we have are treasure maps.'

Arabella's eyes narrowed.

'You're telling me you set off across huge expanses

186

of ocean without the first clue where the rocks are?'

'We're pirates,' Bert snapped. 'We don't need charts.'

'Well, go on then, show me,' Arabella said, waving her hands towards the open sea. 'Show me where the rocks are and Pirate Vic can steer us around.'

I cleared my throat.

'Mum and Dad normally do the navigating. And it's easy for them. They have the Blighty Bling.'

'But we don't have the Blighty Bling. So what are we going to do?'

I had no idea.

Without the Blighty Bling we were completely useless. Even if we had a map, we wouldn't have known how to read it. Without the Blighty Bling we may as well live in a leaky caravan on the south coast. We weren't fit to be at sea.

The sea was churning and my arms ached. I couldn't hold the boat here for much longer.

Behind us, back in the cave, we could hear voices. Loud voices.

'They're coming,' said Bert.

The voices got louder.

Soon I could just see Captain Guillemot approaching. He was standing behind his ship's wheel. Beefster was rowing the boat. Bones and Cath were holding enormous cutlasses.

I looked back at the sea, hoping that a miracle would happen and I would suddenly be able to see the way through.

But the rocks were hidden beneath the waves.

I looked at the others to see if they were as scared as I was. Arabella was shaking, George was crying, Bert was scowling, which I know is his frightened face, and Maud was . . .

. . . Maud was SMILING.

'Vic,' she said, grinning from ear to ear.

'Not NOW, Maud!'

'But Vic,' said Maud. 'I've been a very, very good girl.'

'I said NOT NOW, MAUD.'

'But Vic, I've been really extremely good.'

Maud pointed at her bottom and grinned.

'I got a big, full nappy.'

CHAPTER
21

Mum always tells Maud she is a good girl when she needs her nappy changing. I don't know why. In my opinion there's nothing clever about filling a nappy. Especially when someone is far too old for nappies, like Maud is.

'Maud,' I said. 'This is not the time for a nappy change and I'm bloomin' well not changing it.'

'Nor am I,' Bert spluttered.

Arabella and George looked away and held their noses.

But Maud lay on the floor and howled. She

howled until the boat started to rock. She kicked the deck and shook the mast.

Soon we were wobbling so much I couldn't even think about steering through the rocks.

I looked at Bert.

There wasn't time to have a fight about it.

We ended up changing Maud's nappy, together.

Pirate nappies are made out of old bandanas; they're trickier than the ones you buy at the shops. I held Maud down. Bert undid the knots.

We both held our noses.

But instead we both got a big surprise.

'Wow!' I gasped.

'Blimey,' gulped Bert.

'Oh my giddy aunt!' said Arabella.

Maud cackled loudly.

'I tolded you!' she shouted happily. 'Maud is a VERY good girl!'

And I must say I had to agree with her.

Because lying in the middle of Maud's nappy was . . .

...the Blighty Bling!

Bert spluttered, wiping the Blighty Bling on his trousers and holding it up in the sun. 'Maud, you're a genius! You're the brainiest baby in south-east England. You're a demon, you're . . . You're a blinking fine pirate, that's what you are.'

'But Maud,' I asked. 'How did you get it?'

Maud beamed.

'He stoled it from me,' she cackled. 'So I stoled it back.'

'Stole, not stoled,' corrected Arabella.

Maud stuck out her tongue.

'But Maud,' I said. 'How?'

Maud grinned from ear to ear.

'He putted it in the pocket of his fancy schmancy jacket,' she explained. 'And I goddit.'

So that's why Maud had been so keen to go back for Guillemot's waistcoat. And that's why Guillemot was so worried about her taking it. Maud must have found the Blighty Bling in the pocket and shoved it in her nappy just before we pulled her to safety.

I have to admit it was pretty clever of her.

She was one very brave three-year-old. Bert and I both went to hug her at the same time.

Maud was about to start telling us the story all over again.

So I stuck a strawberry sherbet in her mouth.

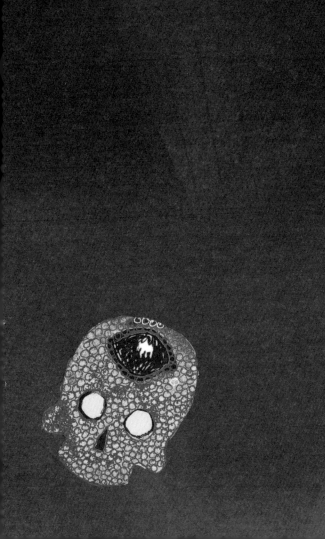

CHAPTER 22

I held the Blighty Bling high in the air and steered *Sixpoint Sally* towards the mainland.

As if by magic, sharp-shaped rocks started to appear through the top of the churning sea. And soon we could see a narrow passage of clear water opening up between the rocks.

'There it is,' gasped Bert. 'That's the way out.'

I pointed *Sixpoint Sally* up the gully.

The rocks disappeared back under the surface as we sailed past them. This was excellent news because it meant Captain Guillemot couldn't follow us out.

Not that this stopped him trying. He threw his map overboard and raced after us anyway.

And hit a rock.

A large hole appeared in *The Raven*'s hull. Water started to pour in. But even this didn't stop Captain Guillemot.

'Haul in the main sail!' I shouted at Bert. 'We need to go faster!'

Bert looked behind, took a big gulp and pulled hard on the main sail – tightening it against the wind to help us gather speed.

'Bert!' I gulped. 'Hurry!'

For once Bert didn't answer back. He was too busy hoisting and pulling in sails. I have to admit he was doing a good job too. But the gully through the rocks was getting narrower.

'Slow down!' called Arabella from the bow. 'You only just missed that rock.'

'Keep doing what you're doing, Vic,' said Bert. Which actually made me feel quite good. After all, Bert was the only one on board who knew how hard it was to sail a large ship through a narrow gully.

The tide was falling fast. If it we didn't hit deeper water soon, we were going to run aground.

Behind us, despite the huge hole in her hull, *The Raven* was closing in on us.

Maud stuck out her tongue at Captain Guillemot and shouted, 'Die, die!' at the top of her voice. But I couldn't laugh. Not yet. I could still see a few more rocks between us and the open sea. I couldn't relax until we were safely through.

'Hoist the jib!' I told Bert. 'We need more speed!'

With the extra sail up, we scudded through the last of the rocks into the open sea.

'We've done it!' I laughed, turning to the others and jumping up and down. 'We're free.'

Then everything went black.

CHAPTER 23

'Wake up!' shouted a cross-sounding voice. 'Wake up, right now!'

'I told you she was faking,' shouted someone else.

Then I felt two large hands pull me up.

He's got us, I thought. We'd been so close to getting away but in the end we hadn't made it. I didn't even feel frightened, I just felt sad.

Sad that I'd failed to look after my little sister, sad that I'd failed to rescue the family ship, sad that I'd failed to defend the family honour. Sad, even, that I'd never be able to fight Bert again.

Dad may have lost our boat over a game of cards, but we'd managed to lose her for a second time – and we'd lost the Blighty Bling too.

'Give her something to suck on,' said the cross-sounding voice again.

I braced myself for one of Captain Guillemot's latest forms of torture and suddenly something small and round was shoved into my mouth. *Poison!*

I expected to feel sick straight away. But I didn't feel sick, I felt a bit better. And the poison didn't taste like poison. It tasted of . . .

. . . strawberry sherbet.

I opened my eyes, expecting to see the huge hairy face of Captain Guillemot.

But instead I saw white-blond hair, big brown eyes and rosy-red lips surrounding a rotten-tooth grin.

'Maud!'

Maud leaped into my arms and bit me on the cheek. Behind Maud, three other faces stared at me.

'She lives to see another day,' said Arabella.

George patted me on the back and smiled again. He was getting more smiley by the minute.

Bert asked why I had to wake up just when he was getting some peace. But I know he didn't mean it because when he held out his hand to help me up it was shaking quite a lot and his face had gone pale.

I couldn't work out why they weren't tied up.

'Haven't we been captured?'

'Captured?' said Bert. 'We're McScurvys. We don't get captured.'

I looked from side to side. I could see blue water surrounding us. We were sailing along in the middle of the sea. And bobbing along behind us, tied to a long piece of rope, were the boats we'd stolen (well, borrowed) all those hours ago.

'But . . .'

'You jumped so high, the boom swung round

203

and hit you on the head. You were knocked out cold. We picked up the other boats without you.'

'Knocked out?' I gasped. Slowly it was beginning to make sense. I shook my head as if to knock my brain back into position but there was one thing still bothering me.

'What about Guillemot?' I asked in a whisper.

Arabella smiled, '*The Raven* got wrecked. You should have heard Guillemot's roars.'

I shook my head. This was excellent news.

'And we're on our way home?'

Arabella, Bert, George and Maud all grinned. They put the Blighty Bling around my neck. 'Aye aye, Captain,' they said. 'We're on our way home.'

CHAPTER
24

The Blighty Bling showed us the way back.

We sailed through churning sea. We avoided rocks and whirlpools. We raced dolphins and flying fish. We listened to the howl of the gale.

Then the wind died down, the water became flatter and I could smell the best thing in the world – fish and chips. I spotted the beach we'd left all those hours ago. There were the breakwaters and the shut-down cafés, the rubbish floating in the sea. If I squinted, I could just make out our family caravan wobbling in the breeze.

Everything looked normal and yet . . .

. . . something felt different.

I looked around at the others.

Arabella and George were still wearing their silly dressing-up clothes, they looked exactly the same as when we'd met them on the beach this morning. Except . . .

. . . they didn't look like children dressing up as pirates. They looked like real pirates.

We all did.

That's what had changed.

The smell of fish and chips grew stronger. I picked up Arabella's telescope.

In the distance I spotted Mum and Dad walking back towards our caravan. They were carrying bags full of shopping. I could see crisps and iced buns and a large cake with frosted icing. I could see a jar of strawberry sherbets. I could see chocolate bars and packs of raspberry bubblegum. I could see cookies and caramel fudge and bottles of fizzy drinks.

My tummy started to rumble.

Suddenly I couldn't wait to get home. I couldn't wait to see Mum and Dad's faces when we led them down to the beach to see their old pirate ship anchored in the bay. I couldn't wait to tell them we knew the truth about what had happened to *Sixpoint Sally*. I couldn't wait to tell them that it didn't matter any more. I couldn't wait to put the Blighty Bling safely back in its pink velvet box. I couldn't wait to eat all that food.

The McScurvys were back and we were better than ever. It was time to celebrate.

'What are you smiling about?' asked Arabella.

I was jolted out of my daydream.

'Oh,' I said. 'I was just thinking about the feast we're going to have on the beach tonight. Pirate parties are the best.'

'Well, you'd better not make too much noise or the neighbours will complain,' said Arabella. 'People round here don't tend to have all-night beach parties. People round here are responsible citizens. Noise pollution is a criminal offence.'

I couldn't believe my ears. Arabella had gone

back to being bossy and boring and sensible.

Bert and I stared at her.

'Aren't you coming to the feast?' asked Bert.

'We can't,' said Arabella. 'George and I have to pack Dad's boat safely away then we have to go straight home for supper. Then we need to have our bath, do our homework and go to bed. After all, we've got school tomorrow.'

'But . . .' said Bert. He shook his head. He was too disappointed to speak.

So was I.

A few minutes ago we'd felt like a proper pirate crew. Now Arabella and George were going to return to their normal, boring lives as if today hadn't even happened. We may as well have dreamed the whole thing.

I didn't feel like partying any more.

I didn't feel like stuffing my face with delicious food.

I turned away.

Then I heard a strange sound.

'YO HO HO!' it went. 'YO HO HO!

YO HO HO HO! YO HO HO HO HO!'

You didn't have to be a genius to know what it was. It was pirate laughter and it was coming from right behind me.

Bert and I spun round.

Arabella and George were doubled over with giggles.

Arabella was laughing so much she was hiccupping.

'Did you really think we'd choose a healthy supper and homework over a proper pirate feast?' she said, tears of laughter streaming down her face. 'I was JUST JOKING, you big bandanas. Of course we're coming to the party. We don't care if we're late home. We don't care about homework. We don't care if we get in trouble (well, not this once anyway). We're pirates now – and don't you forget it!'

'Shiver me timbers!' I whispered, the smile returning to my face.

'You old sea dog,' said Bert, chuckling.

'Farty pants!' shouted Maud, kissing George twenty-seven times.

I have to admit it was EXTREMELY piratey of them to trick us like that. It was just the sort of thing you'd expect from Captain Blackbird and Swashbuckler Robin.

The sun fell slowly out of the sky like a huge fiery yo-yo. It turned our faces orange and pink. It lit up the sea.

We sang shanties at the tops of our voices. We taught Pedro to say more rude words. We crunched strawberry sherbets. We burped. We laughed and we laughed and we laughed.

The End